CHAUCER'S TEAM

Performance anxiety on and off the cricket field

By Stephen Quinn

Dedicated to cricket tragics around the
world, and the people who love them

INTRODUCTION

IN APRIL, men's thoughts turn to the new cricket season. The weather may be gloomy but in their hearts and memories the sun shines on emerald fields and the sky is always blue. Their bodies yearn for the stretch of sinew. Perhaps goaded by memories of previous success or failure, they reflect on fixtures to be arranged and revenges to be taken.

A holy longing for the smell of linseed oil and liniment overwhelms their being. They buy new whites and resurrect gear from musty cupboards. The moth emerges from the chrysalis of winter, resplendent in white and ready to take the field.

Let me introduce the **Pilgrims** cricket team, an odd collection of individuals brought together through necessity and fate. We have no home ground but prefer, like cuckoos, to invade the nests of other teams. Our real home is the Canterbury Tales public house in west London. The pub is our clubhouse – a place of solace and communion. You can share a pint with someone from the team any day or night of the week.

My name is Jeff Chaucer and I captain this team. You don't need to know much about me. I'm a bit too old and stiff to play much, though I once was good enough to get a trial with a county. That was a long time ago. Most of the time I like to watch. I play when needed. That happens all too often with this lot. They are a miserable and magnificent crew, a cross section of English manhood in all its glory and tedium. That last bit was meant to be ironic, by the way. With luck you will acquire a taste for my sense of humour, in the way that people learn to appreciate olives or post-modern cinema.

For all their failings I love this team and care about their fate. Over the years I have got to know most of them as individuals. They confide in me. I have the privilege of one of the three professions where people feel safe to open their hearts: doctors, priests and cricket team captains.

In a way I feel compelled to tell you their stories. Along the way I weave a narrative for myself as well as you. Ultimately what you read is my selected version of events. You can only know what I include. Am I aiming to be omniscient in selecting and editing? Perhaps. I accept I'm creating a version of their lives that suits me. But that is the privilege of the storyteller. I hope these tales will show you these men – and one woman – who they are, and maybe help us all know our true selves.

All of these stories emerged in the Canterbury Tales pub. It is not one of those ghastly gastro pubs that have appeared like lice on a chicken in recent years. It is an ordinary place. Jack, the landlord, leaves us in peace. We have some tables "reserved" at the back and Jack keeps a civilized house – no loud music or nasty slot machines. His pub is welcoming and snug. The carpet is thin and a bit grubby but the beer tastes good and is reasonably priced.

Here are the mainstays of the team. Most of us have been together for many years. Sometimes we interrupt each other the way one member of a long-married couple will finish the other's sentence. Amid the inevitable feuds and jealousies we have grown to tolerate and even appreciate each other.

I've listed the team in likely batting order, assuming they turn up on time. Sometimes even that can be a miracle. I've given you – what can I call it? – a snapshot or pen portrait of each person. You'll discover more about them as you read.

1. Godfrey Playford, 64, former lawyer, elegant opening batsman, elegant white hair, opinionated, smoker, fitness fanatic, nicknamed "God", obsessed with scoring more runs than any other human, keeps notebook with running total after each innings, divorced; pompous

2. Martyn Norris, 40, political speechwriter, went to minor public school, boring opening batsman with focus on defensive strokes, hence nickname of "Barnacle", skinny and angular body, asexual with weird religious beliefs, nervous disposition, appalling caller of runs and likely to run you out

3. Denis Waugh, 35, nicknamed "Tugger", bull-like, muscular, massive arms yet probably the most other-worldly member of the team, does odd jobs, not most elegant batsman in a team of stylistic incompetents, but has natural eye and sometimes can produce amazing "cow corner" hits, also spectacular fielder

4. Edward Theodore, nicknamed "Ned", former thespian, age undisclosed but possibly 50, hates Godfrey, possibly more pompous than Godfrey, elegant speaker but ugly batsman, married to wealthy socialite Isabel who adores him, bon vivant known to imbibe more than most

5. Jeff Chaucer, team captain, nicknamed "JC", declines to reveal his age but admits he might be in his mid to late 50s, a stylish batsman and good strategist, a cricket aesthete who admits time is catching up on him, some people consider him a "good listener" with profound views about humanity

6. Joe Malone, 44, wicketkeeper, nicknamed "Memory" for ability to remember cricket statistics, obsessed with trivia, in great demand for quizzes, married to accountant Gwen similarly obsessed with trivia, known to mutter lurid detail from behind the stumps to faze opposition, has physique attractive to women

7. Simon Venery, 38, nicknamed "Spook" because of his mysterious manner and saturnine looks, claims to be medical research doctor, could be good batsman if he ever arrived on time or practised, finds fielding boring, adequate bowler, slightly "dodgy" and known to supply some team members with drugs

8. Professor Cyril Burrtt, 62, retired university administrator with research interest in lewd limericks, loves red wine, unspectacular record at first slip, defiant batsman with similar style to "Barnacle" (they hold the record for the most

boring partnership), refuses to run singles because they are "tiring"

9. Jasper Karezza, medium-paced opening bowler obsessed with Chinese sexual practices, nicknamed "Kinky" because of these obsessions, a hard-hitting batsmen when under influence of Simon's chemicals, birth date unknown but unreliable sources put his age at about 60

10. Howard Johns, 42, has twin obsessions of cricket and politics, hence nickname of "Tragic", possibly worst spin bowler ever to play any form of cricket in England, local government politician, former conveyance solicitor, known to have large collection of pornographic cricket photographs, useless batsman

11. Charles Bean, 18, charming stepson of Ned from his marriage to Isabel, obsessed with being fit and physical, useful cricketer but mostly used to chase the ball in the field because many of the team are "exhausted dear chap", aspiring spin bowler, nicknamed "Runner"

12. Alice Foster, 30, nicknamed "Lager", girlfriend of Jasper Karezza, makes up numbers when team is short, scorer when team at full strength, attractive, sexually aware, does something in television, useful bat, fellatio expert according to boyfriend.

CHAPTER **1**: Godfrey the accumulator

THE first time I met Godfrey Playford he struck a pose reminiscent of a 1950s Hollywood star. Like those stars, he always seemed to be holding a cigarette. As he accepted my outstretched hand he crooned: "Call me God, dear boy," lit a cigarette, and added as he exhaled "God ... as in Godfrey". His voice was dark brown like his eyes and face – molasses mixed with dark rum – and he pushed back a shock of thick white hair with just a touch of affectation.

Godfrey is our opening batsman, and at 64 the most senior member of the team. I can imagine him practising his strokes in front of the large mirror in his law office, pausing to admire his technique before running his fingers through that elegant hair. He also loves the sound of his voice, and once told me he "lubricates the tonsils" with single malt whisky before appearing in court.

Godfrey is semi-retired but consults to a large law firm. His twin passions of cricket and himself mean it's unlikely he'll make it to the top of a profession already over-populated with pomposity. As a batsman he is beautiful to watch – stylish and elegant. He probably had potential as a young player. He also could have been successful in the law, but he took too many days off during the week to play cricket, often at short notice. This angered colleagues forced to take over his cases.

Yet Godfrey never notices the anger he generates. He has amazing focus and one has to admire his supreme sense of self worth. He always arrives at matches early, and I usually find him in the changing room checking his appearance in the mirror. That white hair receives a lot of attention. Godfrey's approach to batting is similarly obsessive. He refuses to take quick singles. Easy twos with anyone else become a leisurely single to ensure he gets the strike. This is important because Godfrey loves to accumulate runs.

Godfrey keeps a notebook in which he records his score from every innings. The team score is unimportant. Godfrey's ambition is to score more runs than any other man in England who has never played first class cricket. He showed me the notebook soon after we met. It is tattered and held together by rubber bands, with a pencil stuck down its wire spine. Godfrey has accumulated more than 100,000 runs in all forms of cricket since he started playing almost six decades earlier.

We all hear stories of people who live on pet food and later donate millions to charity or leave a fortune to cats in their will. Godfrey has that same fixation with batting. Accumulation has become his focus and reality. Piaget's development theory posits that young children who hold onto their faeces – who enjoy that feeling of retention – take longer to evolve their personality. Godfrey accumulates runs like a child with that anal fixation.

Godfrey is also obsessed with jogging and smoking. He will return from a run with a cigarette dangling from his lips, ready to light once he stops. His jogging technique is like his approach to batting: looking elegant remains paramount. Better to take one's time and avoid any unnecessary sweat. He jogs in his designer gym clothes at what he calls a gentleman's pace. When he runs past shop windows he slows to admire his appearance.

After he finishes his innings Godfrey usually goes for a run. I suspect it's to avoid having to umpire or help with scoring. Godfrey returns in his designer tracksuit, orders a pint and then smokes a packet of Marlboro, pausing often to smooth back his elegant white locks. He is always ready to comment on any faulty technique by the batsman on strike, or offer anecdotes of his batting achievements to any team member foolish enough to sit with him.

Is Godfrey a cricket bore? Yes, but an elegant bore. On the occasions I allowed myself to get trapped in discussion I felt sympathy for his former wife. Godfrey told me his love for cricket was the cause of his divorce. "Women don't understand cricket," he said this week over a pint in the Canterbury Tales. "They can't understand the majesty of a cover drive, or the joy of a deflection to the boundary." More likely his wife could not accept his obsession with preening.

Last night we were alone in the pub. Godfrey's elegant eyebrows gyrated as he watched an attractive pair of women walk by our table. The eyes of a scrivener, comparing legal documents? He preened and said something about liking to "enjoy a bit of that". To avoid a discussion about run accumulation, I resolved to get him talking about things other than cricket. Those tonsils were already well lubricated, and he doubtless anticipated enjoying the sound of his mellow voice. I asked Godfrey if he ever planned to marry again. The lines around his eyes tightened and he drained half of his glass.

"Lately I've been thinking a lot about Sally."

"Your former wife? What was she like?"

"I loved her more than anything on this planet, dear boy." Godfrey seemed to be fighting with emotions that threatened to disrupt his composure. That elegantly suntanned face paled slightly, the ghost of a memory flitting across his eyes. "It was that damn pearl."

I sipped my pint and made encouraging noises.

"I married late in life, when I was 48. Sally was 30, and already more successful as a solicitor than I would ever be.

"We had the most elegant life. A beautiful house. Well-paid jobs. Trips abroad. No kids to worry about. The sex was amazing. Sally told me she adored my body. She especially enjoyed sucking me." Godfrey sipped his beer and his eyes still had a faraway look.

"Sally'd been married before to some foreign bastard, and he'd given her a necklace. Happened after he hit her and she threatened to leave him. That was their pattern and eventually she did leave him. The necklace must have been precious because it was the only thing she wore when we were in bed together. A handful of pearls on a silver chain.

"I took a case out of town and stayed in a hotel for a couple of days. At the hotel a woman approached me in the bar. Her intent was obvious. As a single man I would have grabbed the chance, but now I was married I turned down the offer. I was feeling quite noble, actually.

"It was dark when I got back to our flat that Friday night. Sally never closed the drapes and the light from the street streamed over the bed. I remember thinking how romantic the moon was. It was late summer and still warm. I undressed and slipped into bed.

"We had a game. She pretended to be asleep hoping I would take her. She moaned slightly when I stroked her nipples and I felt that amazing zing I always got when our bodies touched.

"She grabbed me. I was still soft, so she went down on me. It was delicious. Some sensations can't be put into words.

"Then she screamed. Fury in her eyes and voice. When she spoke it was like corn being ground in an old mill: 'Who've you been fucking? You bastard!'

"The anger in her voice was scary. In the moonlight her eyes were yellow. I remember the eyes of a tiger I once saw at the circus as a child. 'What the fuck is this', she screamed. And she held up a pearl she'd found in my pubic hair." Godfrey's eyes were slightly puffy. I thought: This is not the Godfrey I know.

"It was like a still life, a horrible tableau frozen in time." Was Godfrey remembering, or creating his version of events? His face had become rigid and hard. "That pearl. It glistened in her fingers in the moonlight. She shouted: 'Fuck you, you bastard' and threw the pearl at me. I've never seen a woman get dressed so quickly. The room vibrated as she slammed the door behind her.

"I needed a stiff drink. I remember the sound of her car wheels screeching as she drove off. She cleaned up a couple of rubbish bins. Strange what you remember. The moonlight made the room yellow and weird. By then I was onto my second scotch. I couldn't get my mind to work, I was so damn angry. The only thing I could focus on was my batting the next day. Drank most of the bottle before I dozed. Had a massive hangover the next day.

"Sally came back late the next morning. I assumed she wanted some clothing. My head was throbbing and I felt awful. I met her at the door. The game was due to start in a few hours and I was wearing my best creams. She looked haggard, just awful. Her eyes were puffy and red, and she asked if she could hug me. I remember I pulled away. She started to cry. Through the tears I heard her voice but it seemed a long way away: 'That pearl.' The necklace dangled in her outstretched fingers. She tried to say more but nothing came from her mouth. I could see bits of foam on her lips. Not attractive."

Godfrey preened, the fingers of his right hand stroking his hair. His elegant face was the colour of those cheap white candles you buy in Asda. It had formed a mask, the way wax melts into a pool at the end of the evening.

"You forgave her? It was all a mis-understanding?"

Godfrey sipped his bitter. "She was crying and tried to hug me. I saw snot on the end of her nose. Some of the snot touched my cricket shirt. I pushed her away. I wasn't thinking. She sobbed and came at me again. I pushed her ... hard. Blood dripped onto my creams. She just stared at me, and all I could think about was getting the blood out of those damn creams. I heard the door slam." Godfrey drained his glass and looked into the distance. "I scored a half century that day."

A few days later Godfrey and I played in a mid-week game. The changing room was small and Godfrey arrived late. He removed his elegant tracksuit and stripped, a cigarette dangling from his mouth. His face and arms were heavily suntanned – deep brown like his eyes – but the suntan stopped midway up his arms. The rest of his body glowed far whiter than his cricket creams. A ghost of a man sat preening in the mirror as he waited to bat. Brushing his hair seemed almost a meditation. An unlit cigarette hung from his mouth. The mask refused to melt.

After his innings I watched Godfrey open that battered notebook. He had accumulated another 30 runs. And lost so much more.

CHAPTER **2**: Martyn's moral decline

MARTYN Norris is a profoundly confused mixture of piety and sexual anxiety. He has always been a seeker, except he doesn't know what he's looking for. Because of his parents he started as a charismatic Christian – those Pentecostals who speak in tongues. Later he became an even more devout Catholic, then slid sideways into various esoteric areas before becoming a Jain. Later he dabbled with Taoism before his most recent forays into Buddhism.

As a boy aged six, Martyn was sent to a boarding school on the northwest coast of Wales. I imagine he went there with bright hope in his eyes. He returned home after his first year with a crippling shyness that has haunted him all his life. The manacles the mind creates to defend the soul. Because of his shyness, Martyn never says much. He blames this for his spectacular lack of success with women.

Recently, Martyn confessed to me he was still a virgin at the age of 40. Initially his religious views forbade him from visiting prostitutes. By the time he was 30, after embracing a range of spiritual paths, he'd given up all interest in sex – believing that ejaculation sapped his vital essence. Who was that French writer who used to say that each time he came he lost the idea for another novel? Martyn cocooned himself in a blanket of spiritual hope and sexual denial. Over time all that latent energy became focused on work and cricket.

Like Godfrey, Martyn has a profound passion for the game. He admires Godfrey's style and elegance but knows he can never match it, so he focuses on defence. Indeed, he only has two strokes – the forward defensive and the backward defensive. Any runs he manages usually come from edges or defensive pushes. Godfrey loves batting with Martyn because Martyn only ever managed singles, which gives Godfrey the strike. The only time they ever quarrel is when Martyn tries to take a single off the last ball of the over. Martyn's nickname of "Barnacle" encapsulates his approach to life. He clings to cricket and religion the way a mollusc finds solace in a rock.

Like Godfrey, Martyn wears the best quality whites. Even on a dull day they glow as they walk out to open the batting. One is well proportioned, and the other tall and angular. From the boundary Martyn looks like a baby giraffe prancing alongside a thoroughbred.

Opposition teams must be perplexed by the relationship between them. Running between wickets with Martyn can be a disaster because of his tendency towards uncertainty. I've seen him run out partners, sprinting past them screaming "No!" After Martyn had run him out the first time, Godfrey took to standing majestically at the other end of the pitch, his hand held high like King Canute confronting the waves. Confusion becomes inevitable. Sometimes Martyn, careering down the pitch, is forced to apply the brakes, turn, and dive to make his ground. Then he glares at Godfrey as he brushes the dust from his beloved whites.

In truth, Martyn hates better than most. He works as a speechwriter for a minor local politician, Howard "Tragic" Johns, and indeed he recruited Tragic to the team. It's a cliché to suggest that Martyn, denied confidence by fate, became the passionate voice of another through speechwriting. Tragic always speaks highly of Martyn's skills, perhaps because Martyn's silence gave Tragic the chance to appreciate the sound of his own voice.

Martyn uses email and SMS for almost all communication. His bony fingers caress the keyboard of his Blackberry all hours of the night and day, and he even tucks it into his back pocket while batting. Sometimes I see him sending SMS while at the non-striker's end. One day he was facing an especially fast and spiteful bowler. After being hit a few times, leaping like a deranged spider, he changed his approach and stood still, at the last moment turning his back on the ball. A Buddhist approach to batting? The ball kept lower than Martyn expected, smashing into his back pocket. The Blackberry emitted a squeal almost equal to the anguish in Martyn's throat. To the cheers of his teammates he "retired hurt" to find another mobile phone.

Last week Martyn emailed to say he was going to Bangkok for a Buddhist retreat and would miss the next game. Buddhism is his latest spiritual quest, and he pursues this grail with fervour. He became a vegetarian and forsook alcohol. A week later I found him alone in the Canterbury Tales, crouched in a secluded corner of the pub concentrating on yet another SMS. His fingers seemed a blur as they moved across the tiny keyboard. An almost empty bottle of red sat on the table. The dregs in the single glass looked like blood coagulated in a fresh wound.

I offered a joke to break his reverie, suggesting that enlightened people did not need alcohol. His face looked surreal in the blue light from the phone's screen and he squinted a part smile as he looked up. Perhaps he'd not heard my question. "How was the retreat? Hope Tugger was not too cheery." Martyn had reluctantly agreed to go to Thailand with Denis "Tugger" Waugh, another of the team. Martyn has a kind heart and maybe he hoped Tugger would embrace Buddhism. Tugger seemed very keen to experience the delights of the East.

I noted a slur in Martyn's voice. "OK, I guess."

"Just OK?" I paused. I always insert long gaps into our conversations, hoping these will encourage Martyn to talk. In a group he rarely speaks, having too often in his life been drowned out by laddish conviviality.

"I need to talk to you. Confidential stuff." His eyes hardened and I could tell I needed to agree to this condition.

"Strictly between you and me." He nodded and I sat and listened.

"Tugger booked a hotel in the red light area of Bangkok, but didn't tell me what kind of hotel it was. My room was pretty tacky. A big bed and cheap carpet. Ugly wallpaper. No mini-bar but several half bottles of whisky and gin on top of the micro-wave by the door.

"Tugger and I met for a drink in the hotel bar that first night. Tugger wanted to try the local beer. The bar was filled with ugly expat men and dozens of local girls. Tugger called me a sissy when I declined the local beer. I was doing my best to follow the retreat guidelines.

"The girls kept smiling. Tugger invited a couple to sit with us. I excused myself and went to bed. The next night Tugger wanted to go back to the same bar, and insisted I join him, saying he needed a 'wingman'. Tugger ordered more beer and mocked me when I asked for juice. I excused myself early.

"It was the same routine the next night. While I was in the toilet Tugger had invited two girls to our table. They were pretty. My fruit juice tasted a bit strange, sort of bitter.

"Turns out Tugger had bought some pills from Dr Simon. They were supposed to keep him hard. But the thick bastard was too scared to use them, so he slipped one into my juice. Within half an hour I was feeling very strange. The room was trembling and I felt like I was drunk. Had this weird feeling in my groin. One of the girls started stroking my thigh.

"It didn't matter that she couldn't speak much English. We just smiled at each other. She really was pretty, I thought, though the bar was dark and noisy. She pushed a piece of paper into my hand. I thought it might be her phone number, but it was her rate per hour. My head was fuzzy and I struggled to convert Thai baht into pounds.

"I looked across at Tugger but he and the other girl were gone. She told me her name, smiled and took my hand. Next thing I know she was undressing me in my room. I could not move. It was like a dream. I noticed money on the table and realised I'd paid her.

"She started sucking me and it was the most intense feeling I've ever had. I remember her long black hair and the white towel she wore. My knees buckled and I fell backwards onto the bed. She followed, her eyes glowing in the semi dark. I had this image of a wolf stalking its prey. I wanted to pray but all I could think about was the sensation in my cock. The throbbing was almost painful.

"I grabbed her hair and pulled her face to mine. We kissed. She was so tender at first, and then she bit me gently on the lips. I lost control. I couldn't think. My hips started to move. It was like I had no control over them. I felt her breasts through the towel and remember thinking how small they were. I tugged the towel, wanting more of her body, and ran my hand over her stomach. She was half on top of me and kissing me and grabbing me. The throbbing went through me like a drum beat, echoing along my spine. It was like a pulse of energy, cascading up and down my body.

"My hand reached between her legs. I wanted her. I felt a mound of flesh. She had a cock and balls! Shriveled, but definitely a man!"

Martyn's flushed face was a mix of excitement and self-loathing. I reflected on what I would have done. Probably thrown her out. Intrigued, I encouraged Martyn to continue.

"She put a pillow under my head and slipped a condom on my cock. God forgive me! Sat with her back towards me and rode me. She was so gentle." His hand trembled as he paused to sip his wine.

"Afterwards I could not move. I kept thinking about my retreat. She went into the bathroom. Came out wearing beautiful purple underwear. As she left she kissed me on the forehead. A mother putting a child to bed. When I checked out the hotel charged me for a bottle of whisky. I told them I was a Buddhist and didn't drink but they insisted. She must have helped herself as she left."

Martyn's face was still flushed as he finished talking. "Remember you promised never to tell anyone." I nodded. This time I was the one with nothing to say. I drained my pint and made my excuses. When I looked back from across the room

Martyn was staring at his Blackberry. His fingers scurried over the keys. What could have been a halo shimmered around his head, though I'm sure it was just the light from his mobile. We never spoke of Bangkok again.

CHAPTER 3: Tugger's Asian education

MANY in the team consider Denis "Tugger" Waugh rather thick. I confess I did when I first met him. Now I regard him more as otherworldly – a child in an adult's body. Others regard him less fondly. Godfrey suggested the Almighty makes up for deficiencies in one area by over-compensating in another. Tugger has the most massive forearms I've seen on a human being. He's a chunky chap, compact and thick set, and oozes muscles. Sometimes he uses his bat like a tennis racquet, swatting bowlers over their head with one arm.

Before he goes out to bat Tugger does one-hand push-ups in the changing room, while holding a pint with the other. Tugger thinks that kind of thing amusing. Does tend to lower the tone a bit, and I wonder if the committee will invite him back next season. Tugger joined the team this season. He reminds me of one of Picasso's bulls. When we first met I remembered how the great Clive James once described actor Arnold Schwarzenegger as looking like a condom filled with peanuts.

No-one calls Tugger Denis. Not since he and Martyn "Barnacle" Norris had a falling out after Tugger ran Martyn out in the first match of the season. In the changing room, Martyn flung his bat against the wall and then kicked a rubbish bin so hard I had to turn the dented side against the wall so our hosts would not see the damage. I was worried they would not invite us back if they knew how badly we behaved. That afternoon Martyn changed the "D" in Denis into a "P" in the team scorebook.

Martyn and Tugger must have reconciled because they recently went on holiday together to Thailand. It might have been because of their century stand that ensured our win over the dreaded Gaities. Martyn contributed 15 painful runs while Tugger swatted their bowlers around the ground. He has no technique but he has massive strength and a wonderful eye. They walked off arm in arm, so I assumed all was well between them.

Tugger has the most amazing hand-eye co-ordination. I once saw him catch a swallow in mid flight while standing at slip. Professor Cyril Burrtt has been our first slip since last year and he's quite useless, but I've nowhere else to put him because he refuses to chase the ball. Tugger stands next to him at second slip and catches anything that goes near our portly professor. Cyril is so large he makes anyone seem athletic.

As far as I know Tugger does not have a trade or profession. He does odd jobs around the Canterbury Tales, carrying barrels. He tried to get work as a bouncer at a local nightclub, but for all his muscles Tugger does not have the attitude you need for work as a bouncer.

One thing about Tugger fascinates me – he seems to smile all the time, as though he knows some special secret. His smile lights up his face like sunshine after a rainstorm. Some team members consider him several sandwiches short of a picnic, but the gods appear to have given him a capacity for wonder – even joy – at the smallest things in life. Was it Bismarck who said that God protects idiots, drunkards and children?

So I was surprised to find Tugger looking gloomy in the Canterbury Tales when we met this week. His face was pale. Not like the radiant Tugger I'd come to know and love. A serene sadness replaced that kindly smile. I thought of the wedding guest in Coleridge's Rime of the Ancient Mariner: "A sadder and a wiser man / He rose the morrow morn."

"What's up 'Tugger," I asked. "How was the trip?" I remembered what Martyn had told me about the pills but held that piece of information in reserve.

Tugger looked up. He'd shredded several beer mats, seemingly unaware of what his fingers had been doing. His leg twitched and his face seemed green in the eerie light at the back of the pub. Usually he radiates rude health and childlike cheer, and when he talks he burbles like a newborn absorbed with its toys. That night, his beer sat untouched and he seemed genuinely reflective. The silence was almost embarrassing. I could not think of what to say, and Tugger just sat looking at me, a sad puzzlement on his face. I needed to fill the void. "Bangkok! What an amazing place. Hope those girls didn't exhaust you. We need you to get runs this weekend."

Tugger said nothing. He tried to smile. I tried a different approach: "You must have had some fun?"

It seemed to pain Tugger to respond. Some people smile because social decorum demands it – the years train us to prepare a face to meet the faces that we meet. But Tugger's not like other people. His heart was winning the battle for control of his face and his heart was sad.

It took a while to coax Tugger's story from him. Tugger told me he was keen to help Martyn get laid. "I figured it might help him relax and get over all those religious obsessions." I suggested it might also help Martyn's batting. Tugger said he'd booked a hotel for him and Martyn in Bangkok's red light area, and insisted they visit a bar he'd read about on the Internet. All of this I knew because of what Martyn had told me earlier.

"I tried to introduce Martyn to girls in the bar, but he was just not interested. Kept going alone to his room. In London I got some magic pills from Dr Simon. Spook guaranteed they would get anyone aroused. They were my backup plan if the girls couldn't get Martyn interested. I slipped one into his fruit juice."

It's not the first time in my life I've heard of a man helping his mate get laid. One can admire the intention if not the approach. Silently I wondered if Martyn's batting might improve.

"After I slipped Martyn the pill, I met this girl and she suggested we go to my room. I kinda forgot about Martyn. The girl looked very pretty in the bar but when we got to my hotel she insisted on keeping the room dark. Kept saying it was romantic. I was happy because she did things to me that made my head spin." Tugger rolled his eyes backwards. This was the first time I'd seen Tugger animated since we'd met that evening.

"Details man," I insisted, happy as anyone to live vicariously. And maybe hoping the talking cure would help Tugger. We needed him to be fit for our next game and I wanted to meet the smiling Tugger again.

Tugger became almost coy. "Afterwards she lit a ciggie. We were still in bed, and it was kinda romantic." His voice faded as his memory took over. "She took out her mobile to check her messages. I could not take my eyes off her body in that weird light from the phone. So brown and slim and different. Then I saw the scars."

"A lot of those bar girls are hooked on heroin," I said. Of course I had no idea what I was talking about, but I wanted to sound wise. Must have read it somewhere in *The Guardian*.

Tugger shook his head. "Not those kinds of scars. Long scratches. Self inflicted. I asked her what happened. She started to cry. At first I thought it was maybe her way of getting more money from me. She said her boss hit her if she didn't make her quota each night."

I knew I needed to keep him talking. "She spoke good English?"

"A kid. Final year at uni, studying English. We talked for a long while. Finally he showed me a photo of a newborn baby. I said the baby was beautiful, as you do, and she started to cry even more. I asked her where the baby was, with its grandmother maybe? The tears just kept coming. I didn't know how to comfort her. She started to shake and sob."

Tugger was staring at me. I sensed he wanted me to help him, to take away his pain, but I felt powerless and he seemed to know it was something he had to endure. He took a deep breath. "She told me she sold her baby. Can you understand that? She sold it!" Tugger seemed to be using all his strength to hold back a range of emotions. He put a cigarette to his lips but didn't light it. It was the first I knew that Tugger smoked. Not that it matters because Jack the landlord gets upset if anyone lights up. I pushed Tugger's pint closer. His hand trembled as he took the glass. The huge muscles in his forearm bunched as he engulfed the glass. But he did not drink, and put the glass softly back on the table.

"What do you mean sold?" I asked as gently as I could.

"She said she sold the baby to a group of local businessmen. Needed to repay a family debt. Do you know what they do? They smother these newborns, and fill the body with a kilo of heroin. Then they hire some young woman to pretend to

be the mother. She carries the 'sleeping' child –
Tugger used his fingers to make apostrophes – on
a train all the way from Bangkok to Singapore.
Takes three days. They put some chemical in the
body to preserve it. In Singapore a ship takes the
body and distributes the heroin around the world.
God knows what happens to the baby. It took me
all night to piece together the story from this girl.
Her version's true. I checked it on the Internet
when I got home. One of the Bangkok papers
published the story. It was a big scandal."

Tugger's face melted as he finished talking.
His strong jaw quivered and his voice rasped. He
took the cigarette from his mouth and placed it
on the table. The muscles in his body still bulged
when he moved, but he seemed to have weakened
– the bull defeated in the ring, sinking to its
knees. Briefly I wondered why the woman kept a
photo of a dead baby. Then I remembered the
cuts on her body. Tugger's voice broke my reverie.

"Do you know how much she got for the kid?"
He looked around the pub and his eyes glistened
in the dark. "The equivalent of twenty quid. I pay
more than that for a round here."

I thought of my own son, and wanted to be
with him. I reached over and gently massaged
Tugger's massive shoulders. A moan came from
his chest and throat. Tugger and I sat in silence
as we sipped our pints.

CHAPTER 4: Ned's identity crisis

SOMETHING about cricket generates intense rivalries. Edward "Ned" Theodore hates Godfrey, and the loathing is reciprocated. A bit like the way magnets of the same polarity repel each other. Perhaps each recognizes something of himself in the other. Ned knows how desperately Godfrey wants to accumulate runs, so when they bat together Ned aims to deny Godfrey the strike. When on strike he refuses to run singles or forces kamikaze twos.

Ned also tries to take a single off the last ball of each over, to claim the strike in the next over. So when at the non-striker's end, Godfrey counts each ball. Near the end of the over he turns his back on his partner, ostensibly to chat with the umpire. Ned and Godfrey are far more likely to run each other out than fall victim to the opposition's bowling. Watching them together is like observing a German and English general during World War One, each calculating how best to stymie the other. The cricket pitch as no-man's land between the trenches.

It is easy to tell them apart from a distance. Ned dyes his hair jet black to look young. The false patina of youth. Ned's mop of raven curls contrast with Godfrey's white locks. Ned's cricket kit is always clean and new. Like Godfrey, Ned wears stylish and expensive clothing. Both drive recent-model Jaguars. Unlike Godfrey, Ned refuses to reveal his age. So we err on the side of generosity and figure Ned must have been around for about half a century.

It is probably the only half century we can expect, because though stylish in dress Ned has no talent as a batsman. Imagine a jack-in-the-box holding a bat and that will give you a sense of Ned's style. Ned assumes the number four batting position as if it were his by divine right, helped by the fact that he's always early and ready to play while other more capable batsmen are yet to arrive. I've lost count of the number of times better batsmen like Simon "Spook" Venery come in much further down the order because they cannot get out of bed.

In contrast to his ugly batting style, Ned plays the role of wise and witty host with ease. He uses his personality and wife's money to charm his teammates. You must let me tell you about Isabel because she facilitates Ned's lifestyle. She has everything: looks, money, breeding and class. While Ned is a good-looking man in a bland and conventional sort of way, I could never appreciate what Isabel sees in him. Isabel radiates a sense of beauty and charm that is rare among either gender: The kind of woman the gods reserve for saints. Often I wonder why Ned lingers in the Canterbury Tales when he has a woman of that quality at home.

Isabel dotes on him, the lucky bastard, and panders to his whims. Ned claims to be an actor and he's had a few roles, but that was years ago.

Now he seems to spend his time at meditation retreats and health farms – the kind of places where they provide colonic irrigations and Indian head massages three times a day – all courtesy of Isabel's money. A few times a month they throw dinner parties where Ned fetes his favourites with superb food and wine. The favourites are usually people from the Canterbury Tales who express their appreciation of Ned's batting talent or mention admiringly how much they enjoyed watching him in something repeated on one of those obscure cable channels.

Isabel and Ned take several holidays a year – but always in winter so Ned can devote himself to the cricket season. So I found it odd when Isabel phoned to say that Ned was not be available for the next game because he "was away". I invited her for a drink. She seemed distracted when we met in the Canterbury Tales that evening. Even after years of marriage she still looks very beautiful, a MILF if Ned had ever given her a child. Isabel has a son, Charles Bean, from another relationship and you'll meet him later. A beautiful boy.

"Jeffrey! Lovely to see you." Isabel kissed me on the lips. "Turns out it was a case of mistaken identity," she said as I handed her a glass of white wine. I'd chosen a discreet table in one of the back rooms.

"What's this about identity?"

Isabel was flustered. She spoke as if I knew the back-story. I brushed my fingers down her beautiful arm to re-assure her, noticing a zing of excitement and surprising myself at how brazen I felt. Isabel's skin quivered like a snail's antenna but her arm stayed where she had placed it on the table. She bit her bottom lip, and tucked a wisp of blonde hair behind her ear with an elegantly-manicured finger. Her blue eyes glowed. Such a beautiful woman.

I sipped my bitter. "Start from the beginning."

"They arrested Ned ... came to the house almost a week ago. He called me from the police station about midnight. He was frantic. I called my brother, our family solicitor. It seems the police had a warrant for someone with the same name as Ned for credit card fraud. My brother could not convince them Ned was innocent and Ned spent several days in a cell. He only got home the night before last. He's a mess."

I resisted the temptation of schadenfreude. Best to focus on cricket. "But he's OK for the weekend? It's a tough fixture. Sidcup at Sidcup."

The single furrow on Isabel's beautiful forehead told me I'd chosen the wrong approach. "Really, Jeffrey! You need to talk to Ned.

The next night Ned met me at the same table at the back of the Canterbury Tales. I was tempted to ask if he'd found a "boyfriend" in prison but remembered Isabel's words. Ned looked pale and his face had a haunted look. He mumbled "thanks" into the grubby carpet as he took the pint I offered.

The captain of a cricket team is a cross between a priest and a prostitute. We listen to confessions and promise never to discuss indiscretions. What happens in Las Vegas stays in Las Vegas. I had no idea what to say to Ned but presumed he understood the rules. I did not need to say much because when he started to talk the words tumbled from his mouth.

"They put me in a cell. The lights are always on, even when you try to sleep. I got there about 9pm and the guards offered me some food. Dehydrated sandwiches and shitty pot noodles. Dreadful instant coffee. The floor was sticky. My feet squelched when I walked. A television flickered in the corner and I couldn't turn it off. I felt sick in my stomach and went to the toilet. The smell, oh God! I felt dirty but I would not risk a shower. No locks on the toilet or shower doors. No hot water in the showers. Towels the size of dishcloths."

"You had your own cell?"

"Fuck no!" The anger in his voice was palpable. "I was there with a range of male and female misfits and psychos. You know when you think someone's talking to you and you answer back, and you realise they're actually talking on their mobile." His laugh was a donkey braying in the distance. "Most of them were talking to themselves. Like a scene from a Fellini movie." He shook his head. "They confiscate mobiles to stop anyone taking photos."

"How did you reach Isabel?"

"A guard lent me his phone. I only got to talk for a few minutes." By this time he'd drained his pint of bitter. I poured half of my untouched pint into his. "Why did they hold you for so long?"

"God knows. Because they can."

"Where did you sleep?"

"On the floor. One big ugly room. Security cameras everywhere. Those damn lights. The harsh kind that burn into your skull. Each of us a got a shitty pillow and one blanket. And a crappy toothbrush with those tiny tubes of toothpaste, the kind you get on overnight flights in cattle class.

I reflected that Ned had not travelled economy for a while. "Thank God it's summer," he continued. "Fucking floor was hard and I thought I'd never sleep. But eventually I must have."

Ned has never been my favourite person. He's a conceited bastard, and I adore his wife. I felt sorry for him but I could not bring myself to offer the warm milk of human touch. His body looked like a partly deflated football. The deep creases in his neck and throat made him look much older than the magnificent black mane of curls suggested. A tear trickled down Ned's cheek. He did not seem to have the energy to suppress it.

"Steady on, old chap. Major game this weekend." Ned did not seem to hear me.

"I kept to myself. Didn't feel like talking. But one woman kept asking me questions and talking. Wasn't sure if she was bored or lonely, or maybe fancied me. She told me her life story several times. She's from Trinidad. Big girl. Almost as tall as me. Quite striking. But after a while I got sick of her voice. She got angry when I told her to leave me alone, even though I was perfectly civil. That night she spat toothpaste over my feet when I walked past." Ned drained his glass.

"After four days the smell of the place got to me. I needed a wash, despite the cold water. Figured a shower might help me endure the place. I was shivering so much I did not notice the door open."

Scenes from Oz, that American prison drama, entered my mind's eye. "What happened?"

"Maybe places like that make you need human contact. She pulled off her t-shirt and our bodies seemed pulled together. I felt her brown breasts squashed against my chest. I was shivering. Where our bodies touched it felt warm and safe. I felt dizzy. I tried to kiss her. Her hand pushed my face against the wall and as she pushed my body turned as well. I remember how her nipples grazed against my back. She stroked my neck. Then I felt pain in my arse. How can pain be so exciting? I heard something drop onto the shower floor. The cubicle door creaked. I saw a toothbrush on the floor. The water going down the plug was pink."

I could offer no consolation. Ned's single tear had dried on his face.

"I dried myself with that shitty little towel and got dressed. When I went into the main room, she sat watching television. I felt numb. Next thing I know the guard told me I was being released. When I looked back she was still staring at the television." Ned looked like a lost and guilty boy. "I felt humiliated yet turned on at the same time."

"Did you report this to anyone?"

Ned tipped the dregs of beer into his mouth as he rose. "Do you think anyone would believe me? Or cares?"

I watched Ned stride away. "See you Saturday?" I called after him.

He raised an arm in acknowledgement without looking back. "Absolutely," he said, his actor's voice booming across the room.

CHAPTER 5: A feat of memory

JOE Malone's nickname of "Memory" reflects his uncanny ability to remember trivia. He's popular when we have pub quizzes, but the rest of the time he's a bore. He can smother any conversation with cricket statistics. We're lucky, I suppose, that it's his only topic so the rest of the time he sits there looking enigmatic. A man of moderation is our Memory Malone. He spends most evenings in the Canterbury Tales nursing a pint, but he never has more than four before Gwen collects him at the same time each night. Gwen's his mousy wife.

Memory is our wicketkeeper and has been known to mutter mock statistical detail from behind the stumps to faze opposition batsmen. "This guy's IQ is lower than the width of his dick," is a typical saying, followed by a silly laugh. Some batsmen glare at him but Memory's physical shape – he's tall and ripples with muscles – probably persuade them from replying. Memory does not so much crouch behind the stumps as loom like a shadow.

He's one of many in our team I would describe as a cricket hopeful: Someone who loves the game but whose passion far exceeds their abilities. What is it the drives these people? A man's desire should exceed his grasp, as Browing said, but with many of my chaps this option is more ridiculous than sublime. Memory may be a pretty ordinary wicketkeeper but his physical size means no-one will challenge him for the job. Much like Ned in the number four spot in our batting order, Memory assumes his keeping role by dint of physical noblesse oblige.

Cyril Burrtt, the second oldest member of the team, believes his seniority and former position as the dean of a university gives him some baronial privilege to occupy first slip. Cyril simply refuses to chase the ball in the field, so I'm forced to keep Tugger Waugh at second slip. He and Memory cover for Cyril. Most of the easy catches stay in Memory's gloves, and Tugger has pulled off some amazing efforts in front of Cyril.

As a batsman Memory manages a sort of short-arm jab that sends the ball in any number of directions. Godfrey suggests that Memory does, indeed, bat on memory because it's obvious he had no idea about style or technique.

Memory knows the current and previous batting averages – to the second decimal place – of everyone in the team. This does not endure him to colleagues struggling with their form. Memory blithely and loudly supplies the numbers as the bowler is running in. Think of him as an "idiot savant" of cricket statistics. He and his wife run a small business doing the accounts for small businesses and individuals. The tax system in this country is so complicated that people like them thrive, especially as the end of the tax year looms. Most people, myself included, dump their receipts and other document into a box during the year and present a pile of paper to their accountant. Memory seems to love finding order in this chaos.

He lives an uneventful and ordered life, arriving at the pub the same time most evenings. He drinks exactly four pints. He knows he is tedious: "I could bore for England," he said over a pint one evening. Sometimes Memory uses his bulk to barricade people against the bar so they cannot escape his flow of cricket statistics. With Memory I must have used the excuse of needing to go to the toilet more often than with any other member of the team. But his heart is in the right place and he is always happy to buy a round even when he knows his generosity will never be reciprocated.

My strongest memory of Memory was at the end of last season. That year Jack, our landlord, had decided – to use his term – "improve" the tone of the Canterbury Tales by inviting some of the local women's cricket teams to use the pub as their watering hole. He had the women's toilet painted nice pastel colours and even put flowers on the tables.

Our last game against Moulscoombe was washed out and we retired early to the Canterbury Tales. On this final night, despite the late hour, most of the people in the pub were cricketers. Memory had had a good season and consumed more than his usual four pints. Goaded by Ned, he decided on a whim to give away his cricket kit as prizes in a trivia quiz. Tragic, like a true politician, became master of ceremonies and provided the questions while Memory acted as match referee. "Who scored the slowest Test century in the twentieth century?" boomed Tragic. "Was it Geoff Boycott or Trevor Bailey or Mudassar Nazar"? The winner walked away with a new, if sweaty, pair of Memory's batting gloves. "Who got a hatrick in the first Test in which they played?" "Was it Maurice Allom or Peter Petherick or Damien Fleming?" The winner received a pair of pads.

Soon Memory had given away all his equipment, including his kit bag. He stood by the bar in his creams, his pint slopping into the carpet as he swayed. I saw Tragic whisper in his ear. Memory took off his woollen sleeveless jumper and Tragic twirled it in his fingers before announcing another question. A buxom lass wore it for the rest of the night. Next came Memory's shirt. His handsome chest glowed with sweat. Late at night in a snug pub the sight of a naked and taught torso seem oddly provocative. Some women started to clap and whistle. Memory surrendered to the applause and took off his trousers.

I cannot remember the trivia question that led to the disposal of Memory's pants but I can see him standing in the bar wearing only a jockstrap. Amid the clapping and cheering Tragic , who was also very drunk, shouted in my ear: "We can make money for the club from this." Tragic took Memory's arm and stood him on a chair. A ripple of anticipation shimmered around the room. I was standing behind Memory as he slipped off the jockstrap. Tragic slapped Memory's buttocks and they juddered as they both swayed.

Memory began to twirl the jockstrap in a pastiche of a stripper. I noticed his wife, Gwen, at the back of the room but the crowd engulfed her. Memory did not see her. Goaded by Tragic and the crowd's clapping Memory redoubled his gyrations. He seemed to relish the chance to display his wares. If wine reveals the truth – *in vino veritas* – then perhaps beer makes shy men bolder. I found myself thinking about what the porter in the Scottish play says about beer provoking desire but taking away from the performance.

Tragic offered his palms to the crowd like one of those American television evangelists. The clapping abated slightly and I heard Tragic's voice: "You've seen what he has to offer. Who'll give me 20 quid to spend the night with this stud?" One of the women waved sheepishly, amid mocking sounds from her friends. She had a quiet smile on her face. Memory turned to me for help. I shrugged and smiled. The evening had taken on its own momentum.

"I'll pay thirty," came a voice from the crowd. Tragic was smiling and his eyes gleamed. The sweat glowed on his receding forehead.

"Forty," cried another.

An excited Tragic adopted the tone of an auctioneer. "Who will make it fifty for this fine display of manhood? All proceeds to the Pilgrims cricket club." Tragic slapped Memory's buttocks again. This seemed to excite Memory and he began to gyrate even more. His body gleamed with sweat. As he arched his back the muscles in his thighs and buttocks tightened.

A bid for fifty pounds came from the front of the crowd. Tragic pounced, speaking at twice the rate of an auctioneer: "Going once, twice, sold to the lovely lady here in the red t-shirt." He clapped his hands and rushed forward to collect the cash before the woman could change her mind. Tragic knows how to seal a deal. Memory swayed as he climbed off the chair, yet his eyes had a look of triumph. Someone threw him a pair of shorts. To the cheers of the crowd the woman in the red t-shirt led Memory from the room.

Next morning I phoned Memory's mobile but got voice-mail. I left a message and eventually he phoned back. We met in the pub that afternoon. His voice was calm as he related what happened.

"I was wasted. After a while I did not care. Gwen and I had been having a tough time lately and she'd talked about divorce. So I thought 'fuck it' and went with that woman. She didn't tell me her name."

I sipped my beer and nodded encouragement.

"She walked me to her place. It was only a few minutes from the pub, though I couldn't tell you where it is. In the pub she looked OK, I guess about 40 but in good shape. When we got to her place she didn't offer me a drink, just led me by the hand to the bedroom. I actually heard her say 'On your back, boy!'" Memory was animated.

"Someone handed me a pair of shorts as I left the pub. Once I hit the bed all I wanted to do was sleep. But she grabbed my shorts. It was dark in the room and I needed a pee. But before I could move she grabbed my cock. I heard a slight click in the darkness like a door opening and ... well, then I just stopped thinking."

I reflected on the axiom that an erect penis has no conscience. "You lucky bastard," I thought as I smiled.

"I remember looking out into the darkness. No curtains on the window. I could see lamplight outside, and the bobbing silhouette of her head.

"A car pulled into the driveway, and glare from the headlights flooded the room. I was blinded but I saw her face briefly. Her mouth was like a giant doughnut. I heard her say 'My hushband' but she had no precision in her voice. I saw her push something into her mouth, but by then I was pulling on my shorts. I jumped through the window as the front door opened. My cock was still hard and it knocked against the window. It was bloody uncomfortable as I ran down the road."

An image of some deranged pogo stick entered my mind's eye. I was torn between laughter and horror. In the end all I could feel for the poor bastard was pity. "What happened when you got home?" I prepared myself for the worst.

"Gwen was in bed. She didn't say a word. Best sex we've had for a long time. We're going on a second honeymoon next week. Things are great between us." His beamed and I felt elated.

I'm tempted to say "thanks for our Memory" but you would accuse me of being trite. Sometimes life just works out.

CHAPTER **6**: The mysterious doctor

THE most mysterious member of our team is Doctor Simon "Spook" Venery. He's late for every match yet always had an ingenious excuse. Spook has the sallow look of a man who never gets enough sleep, and who uses stimulants to keep going – and I'm not talking about coffee. The fingers of his right hand are stained with nicotine, which I found odd for a medico, and his right knee always twitches when he sits. We chat sometimes though Simon always gives the impression of someone who wants to be elsewhere.

We gave him the nickname of "Spook" after Ned suggested Simon was probably a spy.

No-one knows what kind of medical work Spook does, and he never volunteers information. But he is always generous with drinks after the game if he sticks around. We tell ourselves it's a way of getting back our National Health contributions.

As you probably know, we Pilgrims are a travelling troupe. We invade any available nest, provided they have a good bar. But like homing pigeons we always return to the Canterbury Tales. One day in July rain washed out play by mid afternoon and we ended up at the Canterbury Tales a lot earlier than usual. The joys of the English "summer". Midnight found a handful of us still in the bar. Conversation staggered and eventually settled on a recurring theme – tales of sexual conquest. Spook was uncertain on his feet as he returned with yet another round. The raptors around the table spotted a sparrow. "So Spook," demanded Godfrey, "how many interludes have you had?" Godfrey, our opening bat, is the elder statesman of the team. He was a lawyer before he retired and when he interrogates the team tends to listen.

"Or do you simply screw your patients after you've administered a sedative," offered Ned. His dislike of Godfrey displays itself in the ways he seeks to distinguish himself from his nemesis. Inevitably they seem the same.

Spook sipped his beer. The bags under his eye made him look older than someone in their late thirties. "When people have great sex," he said, pausing to push his tinted spectacles back up his nose. Was it a pause for effect, or a chance to collect his thoughts? "When people have great sex, their bodies release things called neuro-chemicals. One of the main ones is called dopamine. We think of dopamine as the adventure chemical. It makes us want to do crazy things." His voice sounded rich and full, the way one feels after too much Christmas pudding.

"Great sex!" chimed Tragic, our local politician, his eyes porcine with beer and delight. "Surely any sex is great." Tragic was always trying to show he was a man of the world.

Spook ignored the interruption. "Dopamine is a neuro-transmitter – that's a chemical released by brain cells to send signals to other brain cells. It's a natural form of cocaine. It gets women especially excited. It helps bridge the gap between arousal and the big 'O'."

Spook paused to sip his beer. He knew how to hold an audience. "You all know what it's like with sex and women. All that time spent with the mushy stuff. Witty dinner conversations. Holding hands. Flowers and chocolates. An investment of hours. What if it were possible to eliminate all that stuff. Go straight to arousal and desire, and even orgasm within 20 minutes?" He took another sip of beer and seemed to be looking around the room. It was that furtive gaze that caused people to consider Spook a bit dodgy.

Tugger suggested some women like flowers and chocolates. Though some crueler members of the team suggest he's a bit slow I prefer to think of him as walking to the beat of a different drum. The good Professor Cyril Burrtt supported Tugger's approach, calling for a return to romance, and proceeded to recite some love poetry.

Cries of "shut the fuck up" and "let Spook tell his story" drowned their voices.

"Scientists have always believed," Spook continued, "that dopamine is the wonder drug when it comes to orgasms. But it cannot reach the brain from the bloodstream. So we thought it impossible to stimulate orgasms by putting dopamine into a pill. Until now."

Tragic had to interrupt. The flow of beer that day meant the music in his brain followed a few beats behind the regular tune. "Are you saying I slip a pill in a woman's drink and she becomes a nympho?"

Spook calmly played that delivery back along the pitch. "Scientists at my university studied couples. The man provided the um, stimulation, while the woman received the pleasure, and we measured the brain patterns of the receiver, using PET scans.

Spook seemed to be enjoying himself. "For all the non-scientists among us PET stands for positron emission tomography – it's a way to measure brain activity. During the build up to orgasm women experience a shutdown in the region of the brain responsible for things like reasoning – what we call executive decision-making. In other words, they go crazy for sex. We found a way to replicate those wave patterns with a nasal spray, not a pill."

The table went silent, which was most unusual for this group. "We figured," Spook continued, "people would pay for that! And pay big."

Martyn's face opened into a broad smile. He slapped Spook on the back. "This spray makes women want to fuck? Where do I get it?" It was the longest contribution the taciturn Martyn had ever offered our table.

Godfrey's face was pink with a touch of purple over his suntan. His voice was a cross between a proposition and a verbal version of Rodin's Thinker. "This has tremendous business potential."

Spook held his hands palm up to the table to ensure silence before he continued. He was clearly enjoying the chance to lecture. "Serotonin is another of those amazing chemicals the brain releases during an orgasm. Did you know it's got the same chemical base as heroin or anti-depressants? Some people call it the 'comfort' drug. It's also the reason men fall asleep so soon after they cum."

A range of sniggers. The laughter of recognition?

"Another of the chemicals the brain releases during sex is oxytocin. An increase in oxytocin after ejaculation is mainly responsible for the refractory period, and the more oxytocin the longer the refractory period."

Tugger had a pained expression, which suggested he was thinking: "What's a refractory um period?"

Ned snorted: "It's when your cock softens after you've cum, and how long it takes for you to get it hard again, you cretin." Tugger frowned into his beer. Ned looked around, anticipating acknowledgement of his erudition. The nearby television seemed very loud. Ned took a long gulp of bitter. Others copied him. The only sound around the table was the reaching of fingers into packets of crisps.

"We wanted something that would fill women with desire," Spook continued, "and keep men hard." He paused. A palpable sense of delayed gratification. "It was amazing, the level of frenzy this spray produced on our women test subjects."

By this time the men around the table were nodding – I'd like to say sagely, but maybe it was more a case of dribbling with anticipation. As a group they were not particularly attractive. Many had privately complained to me of tangled affairs, unhappy relationships, or wives they said treated them coldly. Some admitted in private they were more interested in cricket than sex. Right now they were spellbound.

Ned broke the silence. He did not seem embarrassed at stating the obvious: "You could make a fortune with a product like that. Men would pay lots for something that makes women want to fuck." His face glowed with sweat and he leered as he drained his pint of bitter.

"We named it Pareunia." Spook said, staring into the distance. "That's just a fancy Latinate word for fucking, by the way." You had to admire the way he could control an audience in the distracting milieu of the Canterbury Tales. "We called it Code Yellow because the bottle glows."

"So you could find 'em in the dark," snorted Tragic, pleased with what he thought was a funny line. Tragic's humour is often rather, ah, tragic ...

Godfrey's voice boomed, drowning out the buzz of conversation at the table: "So when's your magic spray on the market?" Ned smirked, but no-one was willing to verbalise what they were thinking. Godfrey complains of feeling "tired" when conversation turns to his sex life.

Spook took the pint from in front of Martyn and almost drained it. Martyn did not react. Spook looked across the room, his face lined with anxiety. "All of my lab colleagues are dead. I'm the only one left. Someone didn't like the idea of anything that would make people want to fuck. That would keep them happy."

"Fuuuck," said Tugger. In this situation it seemed a lucid summation.

Godfrey was more considered. "Do you need protection, old chap?" He continued before his teammates could comment on the innuendo. "I have contacts with the police." Was Godfrey being helpful, or merely looking to protect a potential investment?

I could see Spook wanted to say more ... perhaps he wanted to accuse the pharmaceutical companies of disposing of his colleagues. Sales of anti-depressants are worth billions of pounds a year. It seemed a massive threat to a huge global business. My mind began to speculate. I could see empty malls because people no longer needed to fill the vacuum in their lives with shopping. Sales of chocolate and other comfort foods would plummet. Sales of Viagra or its natural equivalents would soar. Would people watch more porn movies? Perhaps my teammates would join a gym to tighten their paunches. People like Tragic might start using better quality aftershave instead of nasty products like Brut 30.

Shouts came from near the bar. Two women were fighting, fingers entwined in each other's hair. All heads from our table swung in that direction. A group of paunchy men ogling women in the coitus of conflict is not a pretty sight.

When I looked back Spook was gone. He never turned up for any more games, and we never saw him again in the Canterbury Tales. I looked up the word "pareunia" on the web. Spook's definition was right: From the Greek *pareunos* for bedfellow, a synonym for sexual intercourse. I wondered whether the bottle did glow in the dark. On the web I could find no news stories about claims of a sexual wonder drug, or dead scientists.

Spook's last name was Venery. I know the spelling because I compile the batting order. Unusual name, I thought. I could find no mention of him in the database of registered doctors. On a whim, I looked up the meaning. The dictionary defines "venery" as "the pursuit of sexual gratification". Was Code Yellow a figment of a mind unhinged by booze and stimulants? One thing I do know: Tugger, Tragic and others in the team have not stopped talking about that spray.

CHAPTER 7: A portly professor's journey

WHEN Cyril first played with the Pilgrims he insisted his title should appear in the batting order. Perhaps it made him feel important. "It's Burrtt with two 'r's and two 't's," he said, adding "and my full title is Professor and Dean, of course." I smiled as he added "I assume you'll include all my qualifications in your annual reports and compilations of statistics."

Cyril retired last year after a long career as the dean of the arts faculty at a middle-ranking university. He's keen to resume his cricket career. "I was rather promising as a young chap, you know." But that was 40 years ago, I told him. "Good technique is perennial," he replied, shaping to offer a bloated version of a defensive stroke. Cyril's body long ago surrendered to gravity and he is almost as wide as he is tall. Far be it for me to suggest that academics, especially senior academic administrators, do not belong to this planet. But sometimes after a chat with Cyril I am tempted to believe the adage that those who can, do; those who can't, teach; and those who can't teach become administrators.

As a cricketer Cyril is competent, much I assume like his administrative skills. He is a classic academic – someone who lives in his head with little connection with his body. His corporeal being is merely a vehicle for moving his mind from one meeting to another. Our dear professor can offer profound thoughts about the intimate relationship between Byzantine architecture and twelfth century literature. But he can neither drive a car nor decipher the Underground map.

Cyril is profound in another sense. Too many faculty lunches caused his body to balloon. A deep affection for Bordeaux reds and port also contributed to his portly shape. Like many men of his generation, Cyril loves cricket though his passion remains in inverse relationship with his talent. Cyril can rhapsodise about the greats. When he does I love the man for his stories of the glories of Denis Compton and Bill Edrich, whom he'd seen as a boy. As a player it would be kind to describe Cyril as limited. He adopted the same approach as "Barnacle" Norris, our young opening bat.

At 40, Martyn does seem young compared with some of the stalwarts in the side. He and Cyril hold the record for the least number of runs scored in the most number of minutes. That's partly because of Cyril's obesity. He refuses to run and is incapable of much more than defensive pushes. This combination makes him the slowest but possibly safest batsmen in our side. He's a good man to have in a crisis, but useless when we are chasing runs. Given we are often in trouble, it's good to know Cyril can bat around the middle order and rescue us. I've seen opposition sides slope off the field in disgust at Cyril's ability to do nothing for hours.

Cyril insists on fielding at first slip, because it means the least amount of exertion when we field. He has not taken many catches in that position, apart from those that hit his body. He has perfected a technique of absorbing the ball into his bulk. Think of a raisin dropped into a spotted dick. As I have mentioned elsewhere, the professor has two athletic young chaps either side of him. Tugger has snaffled some miraculous catches in front of Cyril, and our keeper "Memory" Malone performs sterling administrative support on the other side.

Cyril loves food and wine, and insists on a bottle of fine red when we meet at the Canterbury Tales, which has an excellent wine list. Cyril's doctor has warned that too much beer increases blood pressure so he focuses on Bordeaux. Under the influence of Bacchus Cyril is prone to lapse into poetry. This happens often if we field second and Cyril's brought along some good red. He's a great team supporter and claps and encourages more loudly than most. In all he has a good and happy heart – the Labrador breed of cricketing dogs.

Cyril has been on anti-depressants for decades. He blames the pills for his lack of interest in the "female gender" or pretty much anything apart from cricket and wine. He's also famous as a post-modernist theorist. After a bottle of red Cyril declaims about Foucault, Baudrillard and Derrida with the alacrity of a young PhD student. At these times he becomes almost inchoate. His sentences are like cryptic crossword clues. When we field I position myself at mid-off, ostensibly to be able to encourage the bowler but mostly to avoid incomprehensible conversations at slip. After his first meeting with Cyril, Tugger confessed to me he barely understood a word Cyril said. Sadly, he also told Cyril, who thereafter proclaimed Tugger a moron.

Last winter the team went on tour to Hong Kong. We wanted somewhere warm, and a friend of Cyril's at the University of Hong Kong offered us moderate opposition plus digs in university apartments. Cheap accommodation is rare in Hong Kong. We duly assembled in Hong Kong in October when the weather was sunny and warm – a nice respite from the onset of an English winter. Cyril's university friend organised games against some enthusiastic but limited local sides, which we won easily.

The level of hospitality after the games was overwhelming. Afterwards the younger members of the team celebrated by trawling the bars of Wanchai and Central. I shared an apartment with Cyril. He would often excuse himself after dinner and go to bed to read. By the time I retired he would be snoring happily in the other bedroom, books at all angles on top of his duvet, his glasses askew on his face. A small mountain of contentment.

One night I awoke in the middle of the night – the male bladder weakens with age – and I used the glow of my mobile phone to navigate. As I arrived at the bathroom door a naked Moby Dick emerged, guiding a slim brown body in the direction of his room. He was swaying and so intent on his mission that he did not see me.

Best to let Cyril continue the story, as related to me over a late breakfast the next day.

"Last night the chaps talked me into going with them to the bars in Wanchai. I was keen to see this den of iniquity." Cyril's face convulsed into a beaming smile. His eyes creased and he looked like the statue of the giant Buddha we had visited during a guided tour on our second day. "We discovered a salubrious bar called 'Burt's' so I insisted we sojourn there. The nomenclature was different from my name, of course, but it seemed the obvious place to go. A chance to offer libations to the gods to celebrate our victories. Inside were phalanxes of scantily clad Filipina – young women who come to seek their fortune in Hong Kong. Many of them arrive as domestic servants but soon seek alternative employment because of the harsh treatment they receive from their mendacious masters. Did you know many Chinese families make them work six days a week, and pay them a pittance?"

The anger in Cyril's voice and the apparent depth of his knowledge of the economy of the Philippines told me Cyril had received some tutoring from that slim brown body the night before. I mentioned what I had seen in the bathroom the previous night. Cyril's smile became even wider. He announced he was planning to marry and take her back to London.

This surprised me because I had always thought of Cyril as your classic confirmed bachelor. Here he was at 62 declaring his love for a woman perhaps 40 years his junior.

"Her name is Petunia. Such a sweet name," Cyril said. It was obvious he was smitten. I had to ask: "What happened last night?"

"After several libations we found ourselves surrounded by numerous delicious nymphs. They were scantily attired and had numbers pinned to their bosoms."

Bosom is such a quaint term, I thought.

"Petunia was number three. That used to be my batting position when I was a university student. She was exceedingly gregarious and encouraged me to buy copious rounds of drinks. Luckily I had my American Express card. She took exemplary care of me all evening."

Inwardly I winced. A man among boys but a boy among women. He was proud to have lured her to his room. She was probably glad to sleep somewhere pleasant because many domestic workers share crowded apartments in that city, sometimes three to a bed.

"Of course one's equipment has not been called upon to perform for some years, so one was a little apprehensive about what would ensue. But Petunia was a very willing accomplice and we enjoyed convivial bliss."

I remembered the sounds that came from his room when I returned to bed after my nocturnal pee. Howls of laughter from her, and Cyril intoning poetry into the night. Cyril entertained her with bawdy limericks interspersed with classic love poetry. The topic of Cyril's PhD had been the lyrical elements of the mid fifteenth century limerick. Fascinating what we discover about people on tour. Professor Cyril Burrtt remains a world authority on naughty limericks and as a young and aspiring academic had published several well-received papers on this subject. Over breakfast I received an erudite lesson both on the history of the first lewd limerick, and the difficulties of matching metrical patterns to rhyme with Aberystwyth. Something about uniting the organs they pissed with.

With as much delicacy as I could muster, I asked: "Did you do any uniting of your own?"

"It would be ungentlemanly of me to disclose too much of our rhapsodic rendezvous," he said. This I took to be code for not much happened in the uniting department. Cyril's antidepressants have diminished his ability to get aroused. Either way, Cyril did not seem to care. The smile continued to caress his face. Cyril had a fine story to take home and it would remain a treasure in his heart for many years to come.

Did Cyril and Petunia ever wed? He and his girlfriend skyped and emailed for some months but the paperwork and the bureaucracy became too much even for a seasoned administrator like

Cyril. The UK Border Agency ultimately won. The relationship faded into a pleasant memory, a palimpsest of a scene in a painting faded into the house renovation of life.

However, the encounter sparked a fresh research interest for the good professor. He announced in the pub this week that he had enrolled in another PhD, focusing on the relationship between colonial literature and cricket in south-east Asia. This means he will undertake several research trips to England's former colonies in Asia where they play the grand game.

Cyril bubbled with enthusiasm as he described his new adventure and ordered a fine red, the folds in his face and body jiggling with happiness. It's good to find a man with passion in his life.

CHAPTER **8**: Jasper's secret knowledge

JASPER Karezza is fascinated by sex. Ned suggested the nickname "Kinky" last season when a range of sex toys and magazines spilled from Jasper's cricket kit onto the floor of the changing room. The soubriquet stuck when Jasper admitted that night in the pub he'd lost count of the number of red light areas he'd visited, and described in lurid detail how he used the sex toys.

Last season Jasper had a range of girlfriends but this year he seems to have become attached to Alice Foster. Most members of the team assume Jasper is aged in his mid 30s. He looks the same vintage as Alice, who's about 30. When Jasper told me this week he had found a way to become immortal through sex I was intrigued, especially after he said he would be 60 at his next birthday. This required a private chat, so I arranged to meet him in the back room of the Canterbury Tales. Our conversation was so fascinating I can recall almost every detail.

Jasper's voice was strong and supple, like his body. He said his discoveries started three decades ago when he attended a workshop about Taoism. "Weirdly enough, I went to that workshop after an argument with my then girlfriend. She and I were experimenting with some sex toys and I slipped a small vibrator inside her. Later we could not get the damn thing out." Jasper seemed about to laugh but restrained himself. "We tried everything. I even put a magnet inside her hoping it would draw the vibrator out." Jasper shook his head and I noticed a brief smile flicker across his face.

"In the end I told her she had to go to the emergency room of the local hospital. My mistake was to laugh. She got angry and kicked me out. Said she wanted me gone from her apartment when she got back. Always wondered what she told the doctor." This time he chuckled.

The look on my face told Jasper to get on with talking about his discovery.

"I enrolled in that workshop to find another girlfriend. That's where I learned all this amazing stuff about ancient Chinese sex techniques."

I sneezed. Jasper smiled. His eyes twinkled and the fine lines around his green eyes made him look boyish. "Do you know how to tell if a woman will be good in bed?"

I shook my head. "Watch as she sneezes. If she covers her face and suppresses the energy, avoid her in bed." He feigned a delicate and restrained sneeze. "If she is, shall we say, loud and forthcoming she is much more likely to do the same with her orgasms."

"Sounds like pop psychology," I said. Jasper must have detected the suspicion in my voice because he stopped smiling and his voice became serious. "Have you heard about 'eroto-comatose lucidity'?"

I shook my head, thinking: More pop psychology?

"That was the subject of the workshop and it was mind-blowing. They put you on a bed in a darkened room. Dark red sheets and black curtains. Lots of chanting and incense. I was naked and told to lie on my back and remain passive. Three women entered – the workshop leader and a pair of 'aides'. The role of the aides is to exhaust the man while the leader directs proceedings. One aide works on your member while the other pampers the rest of your body. Bloody difficult just to lie there when your cock is being adored by naked women."

I wondered if Jasper was making this up and made a mental note to search the phrase on Google. Later I discovered it's pretty much as he described it.

"The aides use a range of techniques, from focusing solely on your cock to playing with your mind. Lots of sex toys and even hash and marijuana. The aides work as a team. One of them is always sucking you. The other keeps you awake. Their objective is to get you to the point of wanting to cum, but never actually getting there."

The look on my face must have told Jasper I was intrigued and had questions. "They find a pressure point at the base of your cock. They are trained to know when you are about to spurt.

They apply pressure and the urge to ejaculate stops. This stimulation and then suppression can take hours. Eventually you get so exhausted all you want to do is sleep."

Compelling stuff, I thought.

"Just as you fall asleep they find ways to keep you awake. They keep playing with every part of you. Those young women did indescribable things to me. And because you haven't cum, you get excited quickly even though you're exhausted. I was in a weird state between sleep and not asleep, between bliss and oblivion. It's like a trance. What the workshop leader calls the 'sleep of lucidity'. I began to see visions. A bolt of energy surged through my body. It was like electricity, only gentler.

"That was thirty years ago. Since then I've read as much as I can about Taoist sexual practices. They were hidden from the West for almost a thousand years. I practise as often as I can, and I've barely aged since. Do I look almost 60?"

My beer sat untouched on the table. Jasper looked about 35.

"Taoists say that 'ki' or energy is part of everything that exists. The body contains a special form of 'ki' known as 'jing'. Excessive loss of 'jing' results in premature ageing, disease and general fatigue. Once all of it has been expended the body dies. Jing can be lost in many ways, but most commonly through the loss of body fluids.

The fluid said to contain the most 'jing' is semen. Taoists believe if we reduce the number of times we cum we can conserve our life essence and live much longer."

That night I checked what Jasper said. Wikipedia is such a useful tool. "Jing" is the Chinese word for "essence" and Wikipedia says we are born with a fixed amount. Things like stress, illness, substance abuse and orgasm consume our "jing". When it runs out we die. We can acquire "jing" from food and some forms of stimulation such as meditation and special sexual practices.

This conversation with Jasper captivated me. I remember asking whether he was talking only about men and "jing"?

"It works for both men and women. For men, it's called 'cai yin pu yang' or gathering a woman's yin to nourish a man's yang. For women it's known as 'cai yang pu yin' or gathering a man's yang to nourish a woman's yin. The trick is to have one's partner reach orgasm without having an orgasm oneself. This is particularly important for men because 'jing' nourishes the brain. Basically a man needs to prolong the sex act so that he could increase the time he can be inside the woman and absorb her yin essence. Yin is mostly in her juices."

Sounds like a classic battle of the sexes scenario, I said, before I realised from his face that Jasper thought I was being simplistic.

"The major Taoist techniques teach us how to master the differences between male and female sexual arousal, and about liberating and activating the woman while relaxing the man. For men, orgasm needs to be separated from ejaculation. It's possible to have an orgasm without cuming, so you stay hard."

He'd answered my question before I could ask.

"We learn special techniques."

For some reason I thought of our next game. "But the human race to continue, surely the aim of sex is to get women pregnant?"

"Some Taoists say men should never ejaculate. Others provide a formula for the maximum number of ejaculations to maintain health. The general idea is to limit the loss of fluids as much as possible to the level of your desired practice. These sexual practices have been passed down over the centuries, and some practitioners now ascribe less importance to limiting ejaculation. Nevertheless, retention of semen is one of the foundations of Taoist sexual practices."

My face must have told him I had more questions. "How do you stop cuming? We reach a point where we can't stop."

"A man can do several things. You can pull out just before orgasm, a method known as 'coitus conservatus'. Or you can apply pressure on the perineum, the area between the base of your cock and your arsehole. Some Taoists train themselves to separate the impulses involved with ejaculation. It's tricky. You stay inside the woman and clench your pelvic muscles while at the same time chanting a meditation. This forces the 'jing' to the centre of the brain. If a man can have an orgasm but not ejaculate it means he stays hard. My girlfriend likes this method."

The smugness in Jasper's voice was irritating. "Men and women create 'jing' when they couple. By having sex daily we make more and more 'jing', which keeps us healthy. It's one of the keys to immortality." His eyes were sparkling as he sipped his pint before continuing.

"The concept of yin and yang is important in Taoism sex practices. Yang usually refers to men and yin to women. Every interaction between yin and yang has significance so every lovemaking position has importance. Taoist texts describe special sexual positions that help cure or prevent illness. One of the reasons women get so much from sex is they can absorb energy and they don't have to worry about ejaculation or the refractory period." I was glad people like Ned and Tragic were not at the table. They would have interrupted so many times that Jasper would never get a chance to finish.

"In some of the sacred texts the woman is referred to as the 'enemy' because she can cause the man to spill semen and lose vitality. Many of the ancient texts were dedicated to explaining how a man could use sex to extend his own life. But life can only be extended through absorption of the woman's vital energies so some Taoists call the act of sex 'the battle of stealing and strengthening'. You should read some of the classics, like *The Art of the Bedchamber* or *Notes of the Bedchamber*."

I made a mental note of the titles. Jasper had me enthralled.

"Think of sex as a way to strengthen male vitality by embracing the woman's superior energy in her yin. Sex is good for women because her potential yin essence becomes excited and therefore stronger. Sperm is considered one of the most important elements of a man's being, the fountain of his health and vital energy. It will diminish unless it is compensated with an equal quantity of female yin essence."

"Say that in plain English."

"A man should completely satisfy his woman every time he has sex with her. He needs to prolong the sex act so he can increase the time he can be inside the woman and absorb her yin. At the same time he must restrict the essence lost through ejaculation."

I could not resist. "What does Alice say?"

Jasper's smile took over his face. "She is more than satisfied." His voice was a mix of smugness and self-satisfaction. I wanted to slap him.

At almost 60 Jasper still opens the bowling for us, and he also holds the club record for hitting the most sixes in a game. As Godfrey would say, this required further inquiry.

CHAPTER 9: Tragic's spin on affairs

BY NOW most of you have met "Tragic", our spin bowler and local politician. To many in the team Howard Johns seems one-dimensional because of his twin passions: His career as a local government politician, and cricket. His nickname is based on the similarity between his name and that of a former Australian prime minister. The Aussie politician once described himself as a "cricket tragic" – someone so engaged with his team that a loss or even an unfavourable umpiring decision touches him emotionally. During Test matches people like Tragic linger in a corner of the changing shed with a radio or excuse themselves frequently at parties to check the score on television.

Tragic deserves his soubriquet. He has the same obsession with cricket trivia as "Memory" Malone, and the same talent for ingratiating himself with people as "Ned" Theodore. But Tragic is driven. All his life a steely resolve and determination have served as a replacement and bolster for minimal talent. Despite poor grades at school, Tragic found a way to get into a good university where he studied law. After a determined career in real estate law he moved into local government. He epitomizes that quote from American president Calvin Coolidge: "Nothing in the world can take the place of persistence. Talent will not; nothing in the world is more common than unsuccessful men with talent. Genius will not; unrewarded genius is a proverb. Education will not; the world is full of educated derelicts. Persistence and determination alone are omnipotent."

Like Godfrey and Ned, Tragic always turns out well. He wears the crispest creams and his boots are so white they seem to gleam. Because of his poor eyesight Tragic wears glasses with thick lenses. He fixes his spectacles in place with a strap across the back of his head. He chose this approach after seeing a Test player with the same equipment. On hot or rainy days this can be a liability because sweat soon fogs his glasses, making his eyesight even worse. Tragic maintains this is the reason for his poor batting record.

In reality, Tragic is all style but little substance. Some of his political opponents said the same thing when he entered local government. But he's soared above his contemporaries and become a senior member of the local Tory party, and entertains Cabinet ministers when they are in town.

When I think of Tragic I'm reminded of the ancient Greek poets who invoked Melpomene to help them create beautiful lyrics. Melpomene, one of the daughters of the king of the Greek gods, Zeus, was the muse of tragedy. Zeus's nine daughters became the muses of literature. Tragic keeps photographs of current Test cricketers in his kit and invokes their help before a game.

Tragic also has an extensive collection of cricket-related pornography, but that is a story for another day.

Tragic married well and lives in a fine and large house with Fiona. They invite the team to dinner at the start of the season and put on a fine spread. Fiona likes to cook classic English food like roast beef and Yorkshire pudding, or beef Wellington with potato gratin and stuffed peppers. Tragic delights in being mine host. He and Ned get very competitive when entertaining. Tragic and Fiona repeat the dinner at the end of the season, each time supplying the finest wines. Fiona is a pretty thing with a tendency to flirt when she's had too much to drink. During the season she sips Pimms and knits while we field, and organises a splendid afternoon tea. I've noticed several of the team appreciating her attributes, and I'm not talking about her cream cakes. Something about her smile tells me she appreciates the interest.

Despite his enthusiasm for cricket, Tragic is a useless fieldsman. One of the problems of captaining this team is the need to hide so many poor fielders. Thank God for Charles Bean, whom you will meet later. He is like a greyhound, ready to speed after any ball hit towards the boundary. He has been known to overtake older members of the side despite giving them 40 metres head start. But Charles cannot be everywhere. I usually position Tragic near the square-leg umpire. It is a strategic decision. Tragic can use his political guile to build rapport with the umpire, which helps with occasional LBW decisions. Plus the ball is seldom hit in his direction.

On sunny days Tragic has been known to lose concentration. One day we were playing against a fine batsman who had already taken a century off our bowling. Spook Venery came on to bowl and delivered the most delicious long hop. The centurion – eyes bright with delight – pulled savagely towards square leg. The ball cannoned into Tragic's chest before his mind or hands could react, knocking him off his feet. The thud of ball on body could be heard around the ground. Spook was devastated, claiming it as a dropped catch, and howling in outrage. All eyes were on Tragic, who did not move. For a moment we thought he might be unconscious or worse. Spook's howls stopped. It felt like time had stopped until Tragic rose slowly and gracefully, adjusted his glasses, and left the field so Fiona could attend to his wounds. After the match he took special delight in showing the bruise on his chest. For a while he reveled in a new nickname of "Lazarus".

Despite his poor record in the field I've seen Tragic take some extraordinary catches, but only off his own bowling. It'd be wrong to describe what Tragic does as "spin" bowling because that implies the ball deviates after it pitches. Tragic trundles a combination of slow and straight – and sometimes accurate – temptations. The eyes of opposition batsmen sparkle when he comes on to bowl. But they underestimate his guile. Over the years Tragic has learned a few tricks.

During a match against the Gaieties, our sworn enemy, they had us on the rack at almost 250 for only three wickets down. All my front-line bowlers avoided my eye. I remember the reply from Freddy Truman when called upon to bowl in a similar situation. When his captain said "England expects" as an incentive, Freddy replied "No wonder she's the mother country". Yet Tragic was willing to bowl. He got five wickets that day because the opposition under-estimated him and tried to smash him out of the ground. Two half-volleys driven back at ferocious speed saw Tragic snaffle a couple of miracle catches. For one of them his hand seemed to be dangling as if he were adjusting his bootlace, and the ball stuck in his hand. Tugger also took two magnificent catches on the mid-wicket boundary. These would have been sixes on a smaller ground. For one of them Tugger leapt into the air and took the ball one-handed. It was one of those occasions when cricket can be as majestic as classical ballet. Tragic ended with 5-98, off only nine overs. This effort earned him a place on the season's honour board for anyone who scores a century or takes five wickets. Later in the pub Godfrey commented that Tragic almost completed the double — referencing the near century scored off his bowling.

That night we enjoyed many libations in our usual place. Tragic was celebrating his bowling performance and was what *Private Eye* later described as "relaxed and comfortable". The annual Conservative Party conference was taking place in Brighton, though most people in the pub were ignoring the speeches on television. A senior Cabinet minister appeared on the box. Tragic started shouting at the screen like one of those deranged types who hang around public libraries talking to no-one in particular.

Martyn told me Tragic had discovered that wonderful phrase "soft cock" from reading online commentaries about political debate in Australia. Apparently in Australia a "soft cock" refers to a weak or wimpy man; someone who lacks strength of character. Martyn also told me the politician on the television screen had had an affair with Fiona. Tragic announced to the entire pub that the "soft cock" minister spent most of his time at a London club famous for its debauchery. He then proceeded, as the media later reported, "to impune further aspects of the minister's reputation".

Several weeks later Tragic and I were alone in the Canterbury Tales. He claimed the looming defamation case was causing "marital problems" and he wanted my advice. Tragic had consulted Dr Venery first but apparently Spook's medications did not help. Tragic's penis apparently did not have the same desire for Fiona as she had for organising afternoon tea. He ascribed his lack of hardness on the first few nights to excess wine and stress. On subsequent nights the local member still declined to participate even with, shall we say, encouragement from the lovely Fiona's mouth.

But the issue turned out to be deeper. Best to let Tragic tell his version of events.

"Fiona and I went to dinner earlier in the week at my club. We go to lots of political events there. They can be boozy affairs. Late in the evening Fiona was chatting with friends somewhere and I was having a nightcap with Ned in one of those private benches. We overheard a conversation at the next table. Turns out everyone knows what's going on but me."

Tragic is not my favourite person – politicians with too much money and power leave me cold – but the poor bastard was clearly upset. I focused on encouraging him to talk.

"Two women were gossiping about Fiona and Martyn."

"Martyn? Your speech writer?

Tragic nodded. His face displayed its usual mix of charm and calculated control but I could see he was upset. He ground his teeth. "They're ... were ... having an affair."

"Fiona and Martyn? How do you know?"

"I confronted Fiona last night. The bitch ... she admitted it."

I heard someone ask "What do you plan to do?" and realised I was the person talking.

Tragic shook his head. "Nothing." He drank half of his pint and stared into the glass. Tragic loved wine but in public drank beer to foster his image of a man of the people. He seemed at war internally, his better angels fighting with his demons. "A scandal would ruin my career. Fiona has agreed to end it with him. I'm telling you because I know you can be discreet."

Then Tragic rose and offered his hand. It was the dead-fish handshake of a busy politician with much to do. That evening's business had been concluded, and he needed to be at another meeting. The half-consumed beer sat on the table. As he walked away I felt pity for Tragic, a man divorced from his heart.

As far as I know Fiona has had nothing more to do with Martyn. But she does continue to provide excellent afternoon teas.

CHAPTER 10: Charles's divine spark

CHARLES Bean is one of the few members of the team you will not find in the Canterbury Tales several nights a week. Charles is the son of Isabel, and the stepson of "Ned" Theodore. I suspect Isabel wanted to find a way to get her two men to bond so last season she insisted that Ned invite Charles to his games. As invariably happens, some members of the team were always late so Charles fielded for us. Over time he became absorbed into the matrix, and he now turns out regularly. Charles has just reached the age where he can drink legally.

He is a fit and healthy young man. What is it about this age group that they revel in their physicality? I've seen Charles do handstands on one arm. He's even fitter than Tugger, though not as strong. Ned says Charles insists on arm-wrestling at home. I suspect Ned secretly worries that as Charles gets stronger he, Ned, will surrender authority. Ned hates to lose so he tries all sorts of mind games and manoeuvres. Usually Ned's ploys are subtle, like tickling or distracting Charles with a fart or its verbal equivalent. Recently Ned told me, when he faced defeat, he stamped on the boy's foot. Such is the ego of the older male lion.

Charles does not seem to mind. Perhaps he knows he has time on his side. He seems unconcerned about Ned's tricks. Charles exudes a sense of calm unusual in one so young.

I'm grateful Charles is so fit. He fields well and enjoys chasing the ball. I remember that sensation of pursuit of the cherry, though it seems a long time ago. I have a great affection for Charles. He is a polite and thoughtful young man. Last night he asked to stop by the pub for a chat on his way home from the gym. Charles seemed even more pensive than usual. He chose his usual orange juice even though I knew he could have had beer. When he started to talk it felt like he was resolving something important in his mind.

"You know how Ned likes to entertain. He's always inviting people to restaurants and insisting he pays. Mother calls Ned 'Mr Largess'. Sometimes she gets upset when she receives the credit card bills. I hear them argue late at night. Mother gets especially angry when Ned tells her it's only money. She shouts back things like 'Yes, it's only my money' and says how she's tired of carrying him."

I noted the way Charles maintained distance by referring to his stepfather as Ned. He never used the words "father" or even "stepdad".

"Some nights Ned gets so drunk he can't stand up. His friends have to carry him home. Mother speaks harshly to his drinking chums." This last sentence was accompanied by a wry smile, suggesting Isabel's approach was confronting for the chums. "I suspect Ned's friends are torn between their obligation to deliver him home, and their fear of mother's tongue.

"We have two doors at the front of the house – the main one and a wire mesh door to keep out insects. The hinges on that wire door need oil. It screeches like a deranged parrot. I've always wondered why Ned, who can be so precise in his dress sense, refuses to maintain things around the house. That's another thing they argue about.

"To avoid my mother's anger, Ned's friends wedge him between the main door and the wire door. Sometimes I hear them giggling as they scurry away after ringing the bell. My job is to help carry Ned to bed. I dread the screech of that wire door."

I admire the lad's use of language. The sound of the word "scurry" created an image of mice in my head.

"Last Saturday night after the game my mother seemed very distant. Usually she opens the door with a kind of long-suffering sigh and he collapses into our arms. On Saturday night my mother blocked my way as she opened the door and stepped backwards."

In my mind's eye I saw a great tree falling in slow motion, wiping out many smaller bushes as it crashed to the forest floor.

"As Ned landed in the hallway he vomited. I heard my mother say 'disgusting' as she turned away. She stared at the television, and did not look at me when she ordered me to carry him to the toilet. At least Ned stopped vomiting until his head was in the toilet bowl.

"Later as I lowered his head to the pillow I heard him whisper something. His breath stank when I got close enough to hear him say 'my teeth'. I shall never forget that feeling of groping in the toilet bowl. The reek of beer and curry stayed on my hands. I scrubbed bits and pieces off his false teeth. Ned was snoring as I put them in a glass next to his bed. Then I cleaned up the vomit in the hallway.

"To keep my mother happy, I promised never to drink alcohol. That's why I always feel embarrassed in the pub with the Pilgrims. I don't enjoy being mocked for drinking fruit juice. Mother tries to steel my resolve by obliging me to go to church every Sunday. Her brother John gives scary sermons about the evils of drink and fornication. I hate those sermons."

That was obvious from the look on his face.

"Did you know Uncle John is a carpenter? So I asked him once about the best wood with which to make a cricket bat. 'Waste of good wood, making cricket bats,' he said. 'Stupid game played by drunken oafs'."

I wondered about Uncle John, whom I'd only met a few times: A profound mix of righteous indignation and stupidity. Best to avoid discussing Uncle John for fear of showing my contempt for him. So I asked Charles about cricket at school.

"This season I decided to become a leg-spin bowler. But it really hurts my fingers."

I smiled and reminded him that an orange or apple always tastes better when spun 50 times before it's eaten.

The action of spinning a cricket ball means the stitches on the ball cut into soft flesh when the ball is released. I am familiar with the sensation and can appreciate the pain Charles was experiencing.

"My fingers soon had blisters, and the pain was awful. Someone at school said I needed to toughen my skin and suggested soaking my blisters in metholated spirit. I hate the smell but persevered because ...." His voice trailed away before he continued. "One day after church Uncle John visited mother with his wife and son. Uncle John and his son Reg build houses. They both have large, rough hands. Shaking hands with them is like touching a toad, except these toads take pleasure in crushing my hand."

My brain fizzed. I remembered Lord Salisbury's phrase about the "horny-handed sons of toil". It was not meant as a compliment. Charles' delicate pink hands seemed almost to glow in the early-evening light.

"When afternoon tea was over Reg and I played cricket in the back garden. We're not supposed to enjoy ourselves on Sundays but I needed some exercise. Reg insisted on batting. After a while the ball ripped the calluses off my spinning fingers. I winced as I showed the wounds to Reg. He told me methylated spirit was not enough to toughen my 'girly hands'. Said I needed something much stronger. 'You need to piss on your hands,' he said. 'That's what we do at work.'

"The thought repulsed me but I wanted to show I could be tough. Reg's words about being too soft kept echoing in my head. Reg left school when he was 15. He's been working with his father for nearly five years. He seems to dislike the fact I'm still at school and plan to go to university next year. 'Uni's for toffs and wankers,' he said.

I suggested Reg has a small view of the world. Inside my head I heard myself say: "The fruit falls close to the tree."

"Reg insisted I act immediately so I went to the toilet. The smell was unpleasant and the process rather tricky. Worse, the pain was intense. I could not help reacting. I heard Reg sniggering outside the door. Then I saw him holding his stomach and unable to control his laughter. That's not the first time people have taken advantage of me."

I had to ask: "Did the urine help?" Charles admitted that after this incident he did not try again. Said he would stick with methylated spirit.

Charles was silent and I waited for him to speak. I remembered the tricks people have played on me over the years.

"Yesterday morning after church Uncle John took me aside. He told me Ned's brother was dead. Turns out Arthur got drunk the night before with Ned. Arthur decided to take a short cut home through the fields. It was very dark and Arthur fell into a ditch. Broke his neck. Uncle John suggested Arthur's death was God's vengeance on his drinking. Arthur was a butcher and a nice man. I remember thinking how much we'd miss the sausages he gave us every week.

Another pause. Then Charles smiled: "All I wanted to say to Uncle John was 'Fuck you, you miserable arsehole. Where's your compassion?' I said nothing, but I enjoyed those thoughts.

"When I go to university I'm going to refuse all offers from Uncle John to work on building sites with him and Reg. I want to get a job in a library, to be around books. And now I'm 18 I'm going to tell mother that I shan't go to church any more."

I thought about Isabel. She's much more spiritual than her hard-handed and self-righteous brother. John's sermons always insist on an external God who will only be our friend if we remain obedient children. Then I said to Charles: "You must always remember that we are the children of God or Buddha or the Cosmos, or whatever name you want to give to the universe. This means we are all divine sparks. Your Uncle John cannot accept this because to claim to be a spark of something divine would be blasphemy to him. He's probably a good man but he does not understand much. His world is very small and he's undereducated, just like Reg. You know the *Bible* says God is love. If we are able to love, surely that means we are capable of being god-like? The divine spark must be part of who we are."

Charles smiled. He knew this already. I smiled back and said I admired his resolve. He has his mother's kind eyes and smile. He is a beautiful soul. "We could use a good leg-spin bowler. Keep practising. But go easy on the methylated spirit." We both laughed. "You have a lot going for you. Give your mother my best."

Charles nodded slowly and smiled again. We rose in unison. He hugged me tightly for a long time before walking away. As he reached the door he waved and smiled. I knew I was right about that divine spark.

CHAPTER 11: Alice's dual lesson

ALICE Foster likes being one of the boys but remains an ultra-chic mixture of style and femininity. Because of her surname it was inevitable she got nicknamed "Lager". Alice became attached to the team after her boyfriend Jasper "Kinky" Karezza invited her to a game near the end of last season. Initially she refused to help make afternoon tea but instead offered to score, or field when we need her. Alice is quite athletic and like Charles Bean relishes the joys of running around the field. Later she got friendly with Fiona, Tragic's wife, and helps with the afternoon tea.

Alice has a slim body and a mass of blonde curls surrounding pale blue eyes that seem to lust for life. She does something in television though Jasper never told me what. He's more interested in describing her expertise with her mouth, calling Alice a "fellatio fiend". Jasper recently described in detail how she sucked him while she sat on the toilet. He was getting ready to bat at the time. "Man, have you ever tried to fit a stiff cock into the cup of a protector?" In the darkness of the changing room the leer on his florid face made him look evil.

I can appreciate Alice's charms. But I like Alice more for her honesty, and her good heart. Her current project is helping to find homes for Burmese civil war refugees. People who contribute to the lives of others are far more interesting than those obsessed with their own petty jealousies.

Alice is usually calm so I was surprised to receive a call from her today asking to meet urgently. She sounded upset. We met mid morning when the Canterbury Tales is quiet. Alice lives a short walk away. Inside the pub a halo of sunlight streamed around her hair. She looked angelic despite her obvious concerns. I did not need to encourage her to talk, and typically of Alice she came straight to the point.

"You know how Jasper likes to experiment. This morning he asked me to take part in something weird ...." Her voice trailed into silence.

I knew of Jasper's interest in ancient Chinese sexual practices. It was difficult not to feel prurient. I reminded myself to keep this clinical and spoke as calmly as I could: "Tell me what happened."

"Last night Jasper brought a friend home. You know he and I have separate rooms. A room of one's own and all that. He tells me he never cums when he fucks them, so he says it's OK for him to have other women."

All said in a matter-of-fact tone. Did Alice approve of this arrangement?, I wondered. Alice resumed her story before I could contemplate further.

"This morning Jasper was charming and brought me a cup of tea in bed. We chatted and I asked him about today's game. He said he was feeling strong after last night. The fool pounded his chest like some great ape."

I made a mental note to make Jasper bowl lots of overs today.

"Then Jasper asked if I'd join them in his room. He told me he wanted to build up energy for today's game. Said he needed at least two women, and his friend was willing if I was."

I nodded but did not speak. Jasper was indeed going to work hard today.

"His friend's name is Bella. Jasper wanted Bella and me to take turns sucking his cock. But we had to agree not to let him ejaculate. He wants to build up 'jing' – that's cosmic energy – in his body and he loses it if he cums. He presses a spot at the base of his balls and it somehow stops him. Says it makes him strong."

A thought flittered butterfly-like past my mind: Let's test him. I should definitely make Jasper bowl into the wind.

"The room was dark and Jasper had chants playing and incense burning. Bella and I took turns stimulating him. One of us sucked while the other stroked Jasper's chest, to open his chakras." She massaged her jaw. The corners of her eyes crinkled and I wondered if she was trying to play with my mind. "My jaw is a bit stiff."

Alice may have caught the hint of a smile on my face but maintained focus. I refrained from saying anything crass, but wondered whether I could make Jasper bowl from both ends.

"I know you probably think I was foolish, but Jasper insisted. I was intrigued because he'd told me a lot about this tantric stuff. It really fascinates me. He was moaning and writhing on the bed. I could see Bella's eyes shining in the darkness. We worked hard. We both went into a sort of trance as we got into tune with Jasper's body. After a while we were both sweaty. The aim was to exhaust Jasper and keep him aroused at the same time. Bella showed me what to do. When I was sucking I watched her brush his chest with her nipples."

In my imagination I saw two naked and slim young women with Jasper and kept thinking lucky bastard. I wanted to be jealous but all I could think about was how he managed to find women who were into this kind of thing.

"Finally Jasper went into a sort of trance. He stopped moving and his breathing went from heavy to light. His face looked serene. I looked at Bella and she hugged me. I thought she was being friendly, but as soon as our bodies touched I felt this surge like a jolt of electricity and my body started to shake. I've never hugged a naked woman before and I could feel her breasts against me. She started to kiss me. I felt myself getting excited and her mouth tasted good. I could feel her body moving with the rhythm of the chants, pressing against me. I could smell her perfume, and the sweat made our bodies move easily against each other.

"It was so erotic. She stuck a finger into me and I lost control. My body rocked against her and I lost control and moaned. We were rolling around on the floor. I've never been so aroused in my life."

Good thing some members of the team are not listening to this, I thought. How could they concentrate on today's game?

"I lost track of time. We just held each other and our bodies found a magical rhythm. It was like body surfing, caught in a wave of pleasure. It felt as though I was sitting on a warm beach. I swear I could hear waves crashing on the shore. She kissed me all over my body and I heard myself whimpering when she put her tongue in me. I had the best orgasms of my life! Later I did the same for her. We were both moaning and screaming. That's what worried the neighbours."

The pint I was about to savour hovered in mid air. I wanted to know more about the orgasms but forced myself to ask about the neighbours.

"All that screaming. The walls of our apartment are so thin! They thought someone was being attacked. Jasper and I never made that amount of noise. The neighbours called the police. I'd forgotten to lock the front door. Next thing I know a pair of uniforms were standing in the doorway."

What a story for the plods to take back to the station!

"I found bathrobes for Bella and me. One of the officers checked on Jasper and called an ambulance."

What!

"Jasper's face and body were bright red. He had a huge erection yet he looked so calm and serene. One officer covered him with a sheet. You should have seen the look on the cop's face."

I imagined the pole holding up the tent of the sheet. And the look on the police officer's face! But I still could not say what I was thinking. "Are you OK?"

"Bella freaked. Started screaming. One of the cops phoned a woman colleague and they took her to the hospital as well. They sedated her. I planned to phone you from the hospital when I knew Jasper had regained consciousness."

I touched Alice on the back of her hand. "What about you?"

Tears trickled down her cheek. "I originally came to let you know Jasper can't play today. At the hospital the doctors ordered complete bed rest. Said he wouldn't be available for some weeks."

I wondered why Alice had delayed telling me about Jasper's condition. Why had she needed to tell her story first? I repeated my question, and tried to let her know I was concerned about her.

"We almost killed him. Bella and me, we almost killed him." Alice started to sob.

I shook my head as I took her hand. "Jasper chose what happened. He knew the risks."

"That's just the point," Alice said. "Jasper thought this kind of thing, this keeping his energy, could make him live forever."

I shook my head again. "No-one lives forever."

Alice whimpered. Tears trickled down her face. "Jasper was convinced he was immortal. He was always so fit and strong."

Something in the tone of her voice made me listen more intently. "Was? What happened? I thought you said …"

Alice's normally beautiful face was now puffy and tears slipped down her cheeks. "I couldn't tell you before. Jasper's gone. I went back to the hospital to visit him. They put him in a private room with his own balcony. Jasper always liked the idea of private medicine. He was standing on the edge of the balcony, wearing nothing but one of those stupid medical gowns. The cloth was fluttering in the breeze. His naked arse was glowing in the sunlight. He turned to look at me as I walked towards him. Our eyes met for a micro-second. He had this serene look on his face, like he did not have a care in the world. He always said he was immortal. He raised his arms the way a bird prepares for flight, and then he launched himself. I froze and screamed. An orderly grabbed me."

I felt a thud in my heart. The sort of sound that coins make when dropped into a parking meter, and you hear them clunk into the oblivion of the machine's bowels. The coins are lost forever, surrendered to a pointless cause. Jasper was gone? Tears swelled in my eyes.

Alice reached across the table and took my hand. It's a cliché to suggest we were united in grief but my heart united with hers. I looked into Alice's clear blue eyes: "I'll tell the team what happened. We'll organize a wake." She squeezed my hand and smiled faintly before she walked away.

We held a fine wake for Jasper, though his body was never found. The team argued about whether you could have a wake for someone who was never declared dead. In the end nothing was ever resolved but we still drank to his memory. In a way Jasper did manage to become immortal.

CHAPTER 12: A matter of death and life

I HOPE you've come to appreciate the people in these stories as much as I have come to know and love them. To me we are all citizens of the same Earth, and all children of the same cosmic essence. We all possess a divine spark, though many do not yet realise it. How do I know?

Before I elaborate, let me begin by telling my story. I was raised on a farm in the warm bosom of England's south coast. I remember the long hours of summer sunlight. It felt comforting to be warm much of the year. The air was strong with the scent of the sea. Birdsong was part of life. Sunshine and sea air built a healthy body that still sustains me. I was a bookish child and my father constantly teased me about reading when I should be outside. To please him I took up cricket at age 11, and immediately became hooked.

My boyhood memories are strong with aromas: the linseed oil used to season bats, the smell of boot whitener and the tang of liniment applied to aching muscles. As a new member of the team I had to pack the kit after the game, and I savoured the aroma of sweaty pads and batting gloves. But mostly I loved the physical release of running after the ball. My family moved to London when I was 14. My passion for cricket continued. It has always been more than a game. Cricket possesses a special aesthetic, an expression of life's essential beauty. Few places offer more promise than a cricket ground in those moments before play starts. The greenness of the grass varies, depending on the light. An overcast day gives a softer hue towards the emerald end of the continuum. On sunny days the colours dance like the leaves of an olive tree, alternating dark and light greens.

The sky reminds me of my girlfriend's pale blue eyes. The grass bows in gratitude. I sigh with pleasure when I sense the union of sky and field. That unknowing place where heaven ends and earth begins still thrills my being. Then I know we are divine – sparks of heaven in human form. How do I know? I discovered it three years ago. I was in China with Isabel. You've met her before. She's married to Ned. Isabel and I have been lovers for almost 20 years. Isabel got pregnant soon after we met but refused to marry me. I adore her steely nature, the independent streak that refuses help from anyone. Isabel needs her freedom the way flowers need the sun and rain. It is part of the nourishment for the person she needs to become. Isabel and I named our son Charles. Yes, the same Charles who fields for the Pilgrims. With Isabel and me initially it was a convenient relationship. We were what young people now-a-days call "fuck buddies" – an arrangement designed for physical release and fun. But in the past three years things have changed. I've grown to love Isabel deeply and the passion has been reciprocated.

Over those three years life has revealed itself. Every soul is connected to a divine source. We just need a chance to meet that divinity. The incident in China was my chance. I slipped on the pavement and my left knee ballooned to twice the size of the other. Isabel took me to a local hospital where a doctor said I needed antibiotics to kill any infection. In China antibiotics are delivered via injection. A nurse is supposed to give a test dose and wait to check for reactions. In my case the nurse was called away.

I reacted badly. I started sweating, my ears started to ring and I could feel a buzzing in my brain. My heartbeat dawdled like a child reluctant to go to school. I remember reaching into my backpack to get a book to read and then thinking I was dreaming. I never got the book out of my bag. I followed a soft light down a long tunnel and found myself on a beach. The sun was warm on my face and I could smell the sea air. Children were playing and singing. I could hear birdsong and the thwump of waves on the shore. It felt like I had made a long journey home. I lost all sense of time and I was at peace in a place of warmth and comfort. An unbounded joy washed over me and I felt secure and safe.

Isabel's face appeared next to mine. It felt like she was trying to break into my dream. Her voice was blurred. She seemed to be talking to me from outside the room. I could see her outline as if through a pane of frosted glass in the door. The room was dark yet alive with colours. I remember everything with supreme clarity. All activity seemed to be happening in slow motion. I was hovering above my bed looking down on my own body and all the people. In the next bed a group of doctors were treating an old man missing part of the back of his head. His bandages and pillow and the doctors' clothing were all bright red. The room glowed like early-morning sunshine when you open the drapes.

Isabel later told me what happened when she found me. She said I was barely conscious. My voice was slurred, I was soaked with sweat, and my face was white. I seemed to be elsewhere. A doctor was shouting at the nurse who had abandoned me. "The doctor really lost it," Isabel said. This is unusual in Chinese culture, where people control their emotions.

After more than four hours in the emergency room someone turned down the volume of the ringing in my ears. Isabel said my face regained its colour. The buzz in my brain found a peaceful rhythm. A sense of peace and calmness flooded my body. That calm feeling has remained. It's like a message from the universe that all is well and will continue to be well.

Later Isabel pushed my wheelchair to a taxi and we drove in silence back to our hotel. I felt elated but did not need to talk. Colours seemed so much brighter and aromas more pungent. When we travel Isabel is always excited and talkative but during the journey she was pensive. After half an hour of silence she turned to me, her voice shaking: "I thought I'd lost you." Tears trickled down her cheeks. "Do you know that for most of the time in that emergency room you were laughing?" She held my hand tightly. I could feel her fingers merging ever so gently into my skin. Her tears glistened as they dried on her face, and she looked beautiful. I made a joke about wanting to hold her hand when we crossed the street.

Since then I have lost all fear of death. It is just another adventure to face when the time comes. Since China I have come to know a deeper form of love and to accept the divinity of others through that love. I sense what people are thinking. People tell me they feel happy when around me. They seek my guidance and tell me their secrets. I feel their joys and their sadness.

The great Abraham Mazlov used to say we tolerate life with a shrug. That is, we accept the conventions of society but find ways to assert our individuality. I've asked Isabel to leave Ned, but she won't. Says she wants to avoid friction in Charles's life, and she needs to stop Ned from getting half her fortune in a divorce settlement. Isabel is determined to remain an individual. She and I combine our holidays with her business trips. I enjoy those liaisons in five-star hotels. Life has become an elegant arrangement, an acceptance of our unique way of life.

We live close to each other. A leisurely walk to Isabel's apartment takes 14 minutes. We meet for dalliances, as she is wont to call them: Late-morning meetings after Ned has gone to his club or the pub. Sometimes she comes to my apartment. The sense of wonder during love-making is palpable. Like sun and rain for newly planted seeds, it sustains the mystery and joy in our relationship. After all these years I still find Isabel's body exciting.

The sight of her naked back in the morning light thrills me. Her blonde hair flutters over her shoulders like ribbons and I rejoice in the curve of her hips. When we make love the angels sing. Sometimes, alone in my apartment, tears come to my eyes as I remember the beauty of her soul. I know that sounds mushy, but that is simply the way it is. Jasper used to offer advice about sex to the team. But he does not know how it is between Isabel and me. Perhaps no-one will ever understand the glory of the sexual and emotional bond until they know their own god-like quality.

Enough of me. It is time to say goodbye. I hope you have enjoyed these stories from the Canterbury Tales. The members of the Pilgrims cricket team are an odd bunch but we are companions on the road of life. When we meet I listen for the feelings and intent behind the words they speak. Therein lies their true nature.

I leave you with this blessing: May your batting average always be higher than your bowling average. May every catch be held off your bowling. And may you always win the toss in the game of life. Namaste.

THE END

www.ingramcontent.com/pod-product-compliance
Lightning Source LLC
Chambersburg PA
CBHW070449170726

48291CB00005B/1665